The Arizona Connection

Adventures with mind reading and other calming energies

INCLUDING

Adventures in Arizona & Minnesota

&

A preview of times to come

by Noel LaBine

Autumn 2010
© copyright 2010 by Noel LaBine
First Printing

For information contact/ Noel LaBine/ 14263 Crane St. NW/ Andover, MN 55304. 651-303-9264.

This book was printed by.
Publisher's Cataloging-in-Publication Data
LaBine, Noel, 1947-
The Arizona Connection

ISBN: 978-0-9785584-1-3   Musical Comedy Editions

Acknowledgements

This book was made possible with contributions from several people, who were both critical and supportive at the same time; and I mean that in a good way.

Tom Cassidy helped with many aspects of this book's development including layout, formatting, and getting it ready for the printshop. He has also advised me on how to market my work. Tom's support of nontraditional and visonary arts is legendary in Minneapolis and his support of my efforts has been inspiring.

My friend and editor, Kathleen Westberg did a most welcome and thought-provoking editing job. She not only cleaned up the manuscript, but also had me reconsider how to present certain elements of the story.

Diana Ramseyer was encouraging and generous with the space and time I needed to write this work. She also offered editorial advice that helped keep the story on its course.

Also, thanks to Annie of Arizona, who provided encouragement and ideas for this story

To these people, and all others who offered ideas and support, I am grateful.

Sincerely,
Noel LaBine

The Arizona Connection

Adventures with mind reading and other calming energies

INCLUDING

Adventures in Arizona & Minnesota

&

A preview of times to come

by Noel LaBine

Table of Contents

CHAPTER ONE
Treachery in Phoenix

Marie is walking up the side of the mountain. It is early morning and a haze over the valley creates a calm mood. As Marie walks along the rock-strewn path working her way towards the top, she also frequently gazes across the valley and relishes the view. That is one of the reasons why she enjoys this exercise. Suddenly a black bird caws to herald her movement and then flies off its perch towards another place further up the mountain.

By the time she reaches the top, the sun is rising, casting an orange red light across the valley and up the side of the mountain. Pausing to rest, Marie sits on a rock and enjoys the moment.

Craig was on the top of an extension ladder about twenty feet above the ground putting the finishing touches on the installation of the security camera he had worked on for most of the past hour. It was late morning and the sun shine was starting to feel good on his back. He was dressed in blue jeans, long sleeved yellow cotton shirt and a tan jacket with his company's logo. He had a tool pouch hanging from a belt around his waist. Suddenly he heard a loud crack sound like a car backfiring but he couldn't tell where it was coming from. As he made his way down the ladder, he saw a middle-aged man quickly leave the office area of the building he was working on.

The man looked furtively around him and saw Craig on the ladder. The man then got in his car, fiddled around for a bit, and drove towards Craig. Craig was on the ground by the time the man pulled up alongside him.

"You wouldn't know where the other plant north of Mesa is located would you?" The man looked anxious. He had dark hair with graying temples, and a light blue shirt on with a dark tan jacket. He was perspiring.

Craig answered, "Why, yes I do know. I plan on going over there in a moment, since I've just finished working on this building and I have some work to do over there. Who are you?"

"Harry. Harry Stockwell." He answered, "So, could you tell me where it is?"

"Yes. It's at Fort McDowell. Just take Shea Boulevard East to Highway 87 and then go left on 87 a little ways until you get to Fort McDowell Road and then turn left again."

"Okay. Thanks." The man nodded, put his car in gear and drove off.

As Craig gathered his tools and put them in his car, he kept thinking about how odd that conversation had been. He had just come out of the office. Why had he not asked someone in the office how to get to their other location? Finally, Craig took the extension ladder down and carried it into the grey concrete building he had been working on.

The company, NewStar, whose building he was working on, was a small company with only the two locations. The location here in Scottsdale was a 20,000 square foot office warehouse building with the majority of the building being a warehouse storage area. The office area was mostly for shipping and receiving administration. The company headquarters was another building about the same size in Fort McDowell that included the research and development center for the company. They developed and assembled GPS (ground positioning satellite) equipment for the general public use. Although they owned the patent, they had the parts manufactured elsewhere and then assemble them at their headquarters. Because that location is somewhat out of the way, they decided to have a second location where most of the shipping and receiving takes place. They also distributed products similar to their product in nature. Usually there was at least one truck delivery everyday. This was a slow season, and today was an especially quiet day. When Craig walked into the office area to announce that he was done at this location, there appeared to be no one around.

So Craig announced loudly, "I'm done here now and am going over to the headquarters now. I put the extension ladder in the warehouse." There was a silent pause. "Okay, bye." And he walked out of the building, got in his rental car, and drove off. As he left, Craig thought to himself, "Maybe that is why the stranger came over to ask me directions; apparently there is no one here at the moment."

As he made his way over to Shea Boulevard, Craig hadn't noticed that the strange man had been waiting for him and was now following him. When he pulled into a convenience store to fill his car with gas and buy a soda pop, he still had not noticed.

However, while he was in the store a tall Indian dressed very casually in jeans and a light-green sweatshirt sidled up to him and said, "Hrmm. Don't I know you from somewhere?"

Craig paused and looked the Indian up and down and said, "I don't think so?" He was curious.

Then the Indian said, "I'm a friend of Marie."

"Marie!" Craig's countenance lit up when he heard her name. "I'm a big fan of Marie!"

"Me too," the Indian concurred. "Hrmm. And she showed me a picture of you and said she was your friend and she wanted me to find you and bring you to her."

"How very odd," Craig thought out loud. "Is she okay?"

"She's okay. It's you we're worried about."

"What do you mean by that?" Craig was really curious now.

"There's man that has been causing a lot of trouble for Marie. Marie has her friends watching out for the fellow, because he can be dangerous. When she heard he had some business with NewStar and she knew you were working at NewStar, she asked me to check up on you. Hrmm. I've been staking out the place, and just a little while ago I saw that dangerous fellow go there, and after a little bit leave again. I also saw him talking to you. What did you tell him?"

"You mean Harry Stockwell?"

"Is that what he told you his name is?"

Craig's solar plexus was all knotted up now. When he realized that he had just given information to a man that was an enemy of Marie's he was at first angry, and then anxious. "I told him the other NewStar building was in Fort McDowell on Fort McDowell Road."

"Hmm. He would already have known that. There is another reason why he talked to you, and it is probably the same reason he is following you now. And by the way, his real name is Frank Gray."

"He's following me?" Craig felt panicked now.

"Yeah, look across the street in the parking lot in front of that bank there."

Craig walked over to the front of the building and looked in that direction, and sure enough there was a car just like the one Harry Stockwell had been driving pointed towards the convenience store with a man inside it looking this way.

Craig turned around and walked back to where the Indian stood. "Why would he be following me?" Craig was confused.

"I don't know, but I can help you lose him."

Craig's mind was racing as he tried to sort out all the facts he had just been given. Should he trust this stranger? Why would this other stranger suddenly take so much interest in him? He was only going to the other plant. Why would he be following him?

"What's your name?" Craig asked the Indian.

"Standing Bear."

"What do you propose Standing Bear?"

"Hrmm, he doesn't know who I am, so we could just drive off in my pickup truck. However, we have to get all of your stuff into my truck, so when you abandon your rental car, there won't be any evidence about you that he could find."

"Abandon my car." Craig's mind was racing again. "Suddenly, I'm going to abandon my rental car and go off with a stranger." He didn't think he said this aloud, so was surprised when the Indian answered.

"Yeah, but you'll learn someday that there are people stranger than an Indian like me. I suggest you drive around to the back of the station. Hrmm. Do it in such a way that it looks like you are going to just drive around to get to the other side with the expectation that you will enter the street over there." Standing Bear pointed. "I'm already parked in the back of the station. When you get there, just stop next to me and we'll transfer all your stuff, and leave your car. By the time Frank finds out what happened, we'll be too far down the road for him to pick up our trail. I'll take you to Marie."

Craig was shaking when he walked out of the store. He was anxious about this abrupt change in plans, but he had a gut instinct that this Indian was a good fellow and looking out for his good. Still, it was upsetting to suddenly realize he was in trouble he didn't understand and that a stranger was helping him. He walked over to his rental car, and the sun felt very hot. He got in and drove away as naturally as he could assume, and when he got to the back side of the store there was Standing Bear sitting in an old rusty red Ford pickup.

After transferring all of his stuff, they traveled east on Shea Boulevard, and onto Highway 87 into the Tonto National Forest area. Then they turned off at a crossing and followed a trail north into the regions by the Fort McDowell Indian Reservation along the east side of the Verde River.

After what seemed like an hour, they came to a place up the side of a large hill, where there was an encampment, which included a large wikiup, which is the traditional yurt-like dwelling of the natives of this area. When the pickup came to a stop, the dust from the trail blew by before they got out. At that moment a short, long blonde haired figure emerged from the wikiup.

"Craig!" and then a delightful laugh. "You found him!"

"Hrmm, it wasn't hard." Standing Bear grunted. "I just had to look for trouble, and there he was."

CHAPTER TWO
A Personal Journey

Out of the White cloud sky.
A crow flies to the Valley below.
Its cry opening the spirit.

Marie promised to tell Craig more about what was going on, but only after he had a chance to relax and shake off some of anxiety he had been experiencing for the last hour and half or so.

"Take a walk up to the top of the hill and think about how the Spirit has been good to you while I prepare a lunch for us. Then I will tell you what's going on," Marie promised.

Craig agreed. Craig Miller was a 5'10" middle-aged, brown-haired man from Central Minnesota. He had lived there most of his life except for his experiences when he was a young man in the U.S. Army doing long range reconnaissance patrols in Southeast Asia.

For years he had lived a troubled life with low income. He had felt a degree of hopelessness about his life. Eventually, when he was going through a mid-life crisis he had taken a trip to Arizona and met Marie Greenview, a lady from Arizona, who lived by the Mogollan Rim north of Payson.

Just being around Marie was making his heart sing with joy. He so admired that woman. She had been a major influence on him, when he had come out here about seven years ago looking for another perspective that would help him deal with the challenge of quitting smoking.

Marie was a middle-aged lady with a commanding presence about her. The first time Craig had showed up at her mountain cabin, she answered the door with a telephone in her hand. She invited him in, showed him the living room, and then turned to talk on the phone she was holding. He went into the living room area and lay down on the floor flat on his back, because he felt exhausted after a long day of driving and exploring the Mogollan Rim area. After awhile, she walked into the living room, and began visiting with him unconcerned about his posture.

Forty-eight hours later he was changed forever. *(See footnotes).* She touched his heart, inspired him, and encouraged him to claim his heart or soul self. During that process, he had claimed himself, empowered himself, and set off on a series of changes in his life that would eclipse most all the changes he had undergone before.

During that time with Marie, Craig was asked questions involving what he thought he needed, and the result was that he believed he needed a cleansing ceremony. So she helped him design a ceremony that felt right for him. Craig decided to write down everything that was bothering him on papers, and then with sage, drum, and a walking stick, they walked up to a ridge overlooking a valley. Once there the ceremony started and while burning the papers, she prayed for Craig and smudged him with sage smoke while he prayed for himself. Then, he took the walking stick and with her instructions pounded the end of the walking stick into the ground and said, "I claim myself. I choose to live with honor and glory in happiness." At that time a cawing crow flew out of the north, across the sky in front of them, and down into the valley. The ceremony felt complete.

After that ceremony, Marie asked Craig if he wanted to be a Light Worker. Craig had questions about what that meant.

"You'll be held more responsible."

"In what way?"

"You'll be more sensitive to the abuse going on around you. Your soul will have a stronger desire to heal both your body and your emotional past. As the Buddhist is challenged to no longer be a contributor to the suffering on earth, you also will be expected to hold to that standard. Also, you will be held to a higher level of behavior. If you forget and do something dishonest or you behave out of your integrity, the karmic reaction will be much faster than it has been in the past."

"Than why would I want to be a Light Worker?"

"Because part of your purpose on earth is to help others, and in these changing times many are challenged by the changes that are going on and that will happen in an increasing frequency. The Light Workers have accepted the challenge to help others through these ascending times."

"Ascending times?"

"Yes, this time on earth is one of a growing awareness of the full attributes of mankind. Up until this time in history, man has only started to become conscious of all the possibilities that science and thought can accomplish. During the changing times ahead there will be an ascension or growth of consciousness that will make the twentieth century look like kindergarten."

There was something very attractive and mesmerizing about Marie's prophetic statement and Craig said, "Yes, I think I would like to be a Light Worker." Then Marie touched his fingers and a flash of light with images of a multitude of boxes and jars flashed through his mind.

A handful of days later, as he lay in his bed at night, he suddenly awoke and experienced a wonderful Light Presence. As he lay there in glorious rapture, he felt a love unlike any feeling of love he had experienced before. Truly, Craig felt he had been touched by Greatness. After awhile he fell into sleep again and awoke the next morning very excited to continue to grow and experience self. At first, he expected to be able to experience the light phenomenon again soon. Several weeks later that desire grew into a yearning. Later he realized that it was the Beloved Presence that he yearned for.

This series of events had a powerful effect on Craig's heart. By opening his heart life he had opened himself up to the most powerful energy of all: love. In celebration he wrote this poem:

> *What was in that hand light that opened me?*
> *Come back, my friend!*
> *The yearning of my heart is not an imagined form.*

I desire nothing but those beauties.
Now there was a dawn I will remember.
A rooster crows in a valley of dogs barking.
When my soul heard something from your soul,
I only tasted the drink from your spring.
And the current has moved me forever.

He began to realize the journey of self-discovery as a journey wherein he allowed himself to claim his own awareness of life experiences as being the center point of his life. It was not important what other people or other organizations thought he should be. In the end life and the lessons learned from life would be how he would know the creation. Acceptance of this law allowed the creative energy within to unfold and become evident and manifested in his life. Craig was able to experience another level of who he was because he was seeking that awareness, and was open to other levels of consciousness. The seeking attitude was an important attribute towards his spiritual growth.

After a walk up to the top of the hill and a moment to reflect, Craig made his way down the hill and toward the wikiup. He could see Marie's white Chevy van there next to Standing Bear's rusty red Ford pickup.

::::::

The inside of the wikiup had a very earthy feel. The structure had a radius of about 30 feet and the ceiling was about 12 feet high. The frame was tree branches from 1 ½ inches to 3 inches in diameter and a dark green canvas material was the main covering for the structure. In the center of the large room was a raised earthen platform where a small fire was smoking. The smoke went up the room and out of the building through a center hole in the top of the structure. It was obvious that this was the cooking area with various cooking pots and food scraps on a nearby small table. A larger table was located on the north side of the room and a window about 3 feet square was framed on the north wall. The view from the window was towards the mountains in the distance. Craig walked in through the only door, which was located on the east side of the building. The floor was earthen.

There was no electricity or plumbing in the building and several coolers and large water jugs were stacked in an area between the table and the door.

Standing Bear was sitting at the table, which had three platters of warm food on it. There were cooked veggies, rice, and beans. Marie was beaming when Craig walked in.

"I hope you are feeling better and have an appetite," she said cheerfully.

"Yes, I am feeling a little peckish," Craig exclaimed.

So, the three of them ate the food, which Standing Bear blessed. Standing Bear was a member of the Apache tribe and had earned his name because of a vision he had when a large bear stood on its rear legs and told Standing Bear to study the ways of his ancestors. He interpreted this dream to mean that he should study natural ways of healing, since a bear vision can be interpreted as a symbol of the healing way. During the course of his studies of the use of native plants he met Marie and they became good friends.

Finally Marie explained to Craig what was going on.

"I've known for some time that Frank Gray is a rascal," she started. "At one time awhile ago, he was running a Ponzi scheme in the Phoenix area. He took me and a lot of other people for a ride until he was caught. Though he was convicted for those crimes, he still continues to cause trouble. Even when he was in prison, he had thugs terrorizing me and others for the purpose of either trying to get more money or trying to keep people quiet about other crimes he committed. I have friends all over the Phoenix area, and also know some of the people that he stole from before. We keep each other informed about what Frank is up to. When I heard he was going to some of his former victims and trying to extort them out of money, I knew that Sam Beamquist at NewStar was one of them. And when I learned that you were doing some work for NewStar, I thought that maybe someone should keep an eye out about what was going on there. Standing Bear said he was going to be in that part of Scottsdale today, so he agreed to check out NewStar."

"Hrmm. When I got there, I decided to keep a distance and watch for a while." Standing Bear was speaking now with his strong gentle voice. "I sat there in a shady parking area across the street for almost two hours before I saw a car pull up. Frank got out of it and walked into the building. He wasn't there very long, and then he came out of the building and got into his car. I was surprised to see him drive up to where you were working and talk to you, so I stayed awhile longer. After you left, I waited a little bit and then followed you. It was then that I noticed Frank was following you, too."

"Well, it is strange that he was following me," Craig chimed in. "But now that we have lost him, I really need to report to NewStar or they're going to be upset with me. I just completed installing a surveillance system at their Scottsdale plant and I need to report on that progress to them."

"We were just getting to that part," Standing Bear said. "Marie can drive you over to NewStar and I can get one of my friends and return your rental car."

"Hrmm. Why return my rental car?" Craig wondered.

"Because Frank knows what it looks like," Standing Bear said. "And trust us; if he was following you, he was up to no good."

Both Standing Bear, a tall Indian with a large head and a large mane of black hair who stood and spoke very firmly, and Marie were very powerful personalities. Basically, there was no reason not to go along with their suggestions; so Craig agreed.

CHAPTER 3
A Misadventure

When they got to the NewStar facility in Fort McDowell everything seemed normal. Marie dropped Craig off.

"Do you need your tools or anything?"

"Yes. I better carry all of my stuff, just in case."

"Just give me a buzz on my cell phone when you want to get picked up or want a ride somewhere. I'm just going to go over to the mall and get a cup of coffee and do some reading while I'm waiting for you." Marie acted wistful like she was already mentally detaching from the moment.

Then Craig walked into the building and was greeted by some very anxious people.

"Where have you been?" was the first thing that Don Fernando, the plant manger, said. Not "Hello" or "It's good to see you," but "Where have you been?" in a very accusing tone.

"I stopped for lunch" Craig stammered.

"We want you to come here," Don said as he grabbed Craig by the back of his arm and gently pulled him towards his office. "Let's go into my office and talk."

Once in the office, Don closed the door and said, "Did anything strange happen while you were at the Scottsdale building?" The mood and tone of Don's voice was still anxious and accusatory.

"Yes. It was strange that when I went into the office to report that my work was completed there, no one was around. I thought they might be in the bathroom, so I announced my departure very loudly before I left. Why are you asking? Is something the matter?"

"We'll get to that later," Don said in a calmer tone now. "Let's talk about your work progress. What else needs to be done?"

"Well, basically the system should be working as planned now. We just have to check your computers here to make sure that the video surveillance for both buildings can be monitored from here."

"You mean the video surveillance has been working for awhile?" Don was getting excited again.

"Yes. Go ahead and check it. If you want, I can show you how."

So the two of them positioned themselves in front of Don's computer and Don wanted Craig to tell him what to do. They got into the Safe 'n Sound software that was running the system, and then they could see multiple windows on the computer screen that revealed the various parts of the building in Scottsdale.

"Can we look back to see what may have happened there this morning?" Don asked.

"Sure," Craig answered. "Safe 'n Sound has very flexible software. That is one of the neat features of our company's product." He gave Don instructions on how to set the time back to the moment the place opened in the morning.

"Now you can move ahead in ten minute increments until you see something that you want more detail on and then you can watch it play-by-play."

Soon they came to a screen in one of the windows that showed activity in the office with a blonde-haired middle-aged man. Craig instructed Don how to slow it down, and soon they saw the man point what looked like a gun at Beamquist. Then what looked like a gun smoked, and Beamquist fell down.

Don's face turned white as he slowly turned to Craig and said, "I knew something happened, because when no one answered at the Scottsdale plant, I sent someone over and they found Beamquist lying behind the counter in a pool of blood. I'm sorry, but until I saw this video we thought you may have had something to do with it."

Craig was shaken now also. "That's awful," he said.

Soon a Maricopa County Deputy Sheriff pulled into the front of the NewStar building. Two deputies came in and Don asked them to step into his office. There he showed them the video that he and Craig had just looked at.

A husky, six-foot, blonde-haired deputy asked, "Does anybody know who that guy is?"

"No," Don said.

Craig just shook his shoulders. It would be hard to explain what little he knew about this sinister fellow, and there was no reason for him to get involved any more than he had to. He would be going back to Minnesota soon, so it would be best to stay detached.

"Well, we'll have to get a copy of that video to take to headquarters and we'll have our detectives figure out who he is."

Don agreed and Craig showed him how to make a copy of the video. After about 30 minutes, he had given a statement to the police and given them a copy of the video. He did tell them about the brief conversation that he had with the man, who identified himself as Harry Stockwell; but not that he had learned he was disguising himself and that he was also Frank Gray. Then he spent some more time with Don. He originally planned to talk about the guarantees of the system and the customer service plan, but Don was too emotionally upset to talk about those details, and instead he shared with Craig the relationship he had had with Beamquist. Although it was a somewhat detached employer-employee relationship, it was a relationship nonetheless. Craig tried to be a comfort to Don, and stayed with him for a while. Then he called Marie.

::::::

Frank Gray drove over to an address in Paradise Valley that he knew well. It was the home of an acquaintance that he had known for years, Al Mencini.

It bothered him that he had lost sight of the fellow who had been working on the NewStar building. He was hoping Al Mencini would have an opinion about what to do.

The house was a large stucco house in the Spanish villa style with red tile roof. There was a half-circle drive that curved in front of the main entrance that included a large, double, wood-carved door. When he rang the doorbell, a middle-aged attractive Mexican woman answered the door. "Can I help you?"

"Is Al Mencini in?

"Who shall I say is calling?"

"Frank Gray."

"Just a moment." And she closed the door. A moment later it opened, and she said, "Come in, please."

Frank stepped into the vestibule, which opened onto a hallway with a grand staircase that led to the second floor.

"Right this way," the woman said as she led him into the room on the left.

There was a fireplace on the opposite side of the room and to the right there was a large desk with an elderly man with a yellow shirt and a gray cardigan sweater seated behind it.

"Hello Frank. What do you have to report today?" he asked in a matter-of-fact tone that revealed a level of intimacy that was very business-like.

"Well, the deed is done, but there may be a witness that I would like to eliminate."

The old man looked intensely at Frank in a very dissatisfied manner. "Who is this witness and why was there a witness?"

Frank answered, "There was a fellow working on the opposite side of the building, who I didn't think would notice who I was. After I shot Beamquist, I decided to check on who the fellow was, so I put on a hair piece and drove over and asked him a simple question. His response was calm, so I assume he didn't suspect anything. I decided to stalk him for a while anyway, so I could get more information about him; in case we might need it. Along the way, I lost him. I did get some information about him though. At the very worst, he will give a poor description of who I am. Nevertheless, to be safe maybe I should eliminate him, too."

"No!" Mencini stood up now. "Leave him alone. Chances are you'll just bungle it if you make an attempt at his life. Besides, he doesn't know who you are. All he has is a disguised image of you. It was Beamquist who knew too much. This nobody couldn't possibly cause us any harm." By this time Mencini had turned away from Frank.

"Maybe you should just take a trip away for awhile." His voice was growing softer. "Somewhere where nobody knows you. Somewhere like Mexico."

Frank stiffened as he thought to himself, 'Mexico? Why that bastard just wants to get rid of me now. I'll just agree and then do whatever I want.' Then he said aloud, "Okay, that sounds like a better idea. When do you think I should go?"

"Now! What's to keep you here now that this business is cleaned up?"

Frank felt paralyzed. He didn't expect this response, but life at a resort in Mexico would be a lot better than the 15 years that he had spent in prison, and he didn't want to go back to prison.

"I'd like to make a couple of contacts before I leave."

"I don't think that would be wise," Mencini spoke in a cold, steely way that sent shivers up Frank's spine. "I'll send someone to get your bags and we'll get you on the next plane to Puerto Vallarta. Meanwhile, you just stay here and wait."

Frank walked over to a sofa chair and collapsed into it.

CHAPTER FOUR
Change can be a Choice

"Where do you want to go?" Marie asked when he got into her van.

Craig told her about the information that he had learned from watching the video.

"I was thinking I should go back to my hotel room. Do you think that would be okay?"

"No, that's a bad idea. We have to assume that Frank thinks you are a potential witness who can testify that you saw him at the scene of the crime. He is obviously a very dangerous person, and he does not work alone. So I don't think it would be wise to stay in a room that is under your name."

"Well I should go get my clothes and stuff and check out of the room anyway."

"I'll have one of my friends do that for you. That way if he or one of his cohorts is watching the hotel, they won't recognize you."

"Marie, it really does seem to me that you are acting paranoid. I mean, what are the odds that this Frank guy is going to find out my name?"

"Oh, trust me. He is smart and clever too. He could probably have found out who had checked out the rental car you abandoned at that convenience store. Not too worry though. I just have to make a couple phone calls and I believe I can find us a nice place to stay at no cost to us in the Biltmore area."

"Do you want me to drive while you are making those calls?"

"Good idea!" Marie got out of the driver's seat, and Craig walked around the van and climbed into the driver's seat.

Marie's friend lived on the second floor of a comfortable condominium just north of Indian School Road and west of Squaw Peak freeway. Upon arriving there they met her friend, an attractive brunette who was dressed in a flamboyant red and yellow top with tan colored jeans. She was a very brave person who agreed to go get Craig's stuff and check out of his hotel room. Craig gave her his credit card, and she cheerfully went off to run the errand. Craig and Marie walked over to a nearby plaza, sat in a patio area and ordered beverages.

They picked up a movie rental before returning to the apartment and shortly after they were settled in, Marie's friend returned. Craig brought his bag up to the apartment.

Craig was interested to learn more about Carolyn. He thanked her for doing the errand for him and asked, "So, how long have you known Marie?"

"Oh . . . it's been . . . several years now," Carolyn answered as she smiled and brushed her dark hair off her shoulders. "We were both at a workshop, and I *reeeally* enjoyed her energy."

"And I yours!" Marie chimed in. "Craig, this woman is a most amazing teacher and artist. She does these beautiful masks and teaches others to connect to their heart-selves with exercises in mask creation."

"That sounds interesting. Please, tell me more."

Carolyn smiled slowly. "I put on weekend workshops and . . . convince people that they have artistic talent. . . . We all do, you know. Just ask a child to do art and they enthusiastically jump at the chance. However, as we grow into adults we experience many instances where art is judged and criticized and many people begin to tell themselves that they can't do art. I get them to move . . . *beyond* that false notion and start decorating plain white masks that I have prepared for them. The most *ah . . . maaazing* thing then happens. People start to decorate their masks in the most ingenious ways. Next, we ask people to explain their masks. The braver souls go first, and the description of what their decorated masks means to them becomes very revealing about their life stories. Eventually, everyone participates. They all leave the workshop with a better understanding of themselves and a better appreciation of the artists within themselves."

By now the three of them were all sitting down, and the conversation got back to the recent drama.

"But you have been through a lot, Craig." Carolyn changed the tone of her voice. "Let's talk about what you've been through."

"First of all, I would like to know why Frank Gray killed Beamquist," Craig said.

"I don't know the particular reason," Marie answered. "But basically it is a result of having chosen the path of greed. I remember when he was a more gentle, caring soul."

"Obviously he has chosen a path where he has become a doer of evil deeds, but when did you know him?"

"We had a partnership for several years. We bought distressed homes from FMHA and flipped them. Some of them we rented out for a while. We fixed up close to 20 of these homes and made some very good money. Things were going along swell for several years. In those days Frank was a charming, entertaining man, who brought delight to both me and others."

"Wow!" Craig exclaimed. "What happened?"

"I can't give you a particular time when he may have lost his godly focus, because I was involved in an automobile accident and had a head injury with brain damage," Marie confessed. "For quite awhile I had a hard time functioning, and I signed power of attorney over to Frank and he handled all of our business. It was during that time that he started the Ponzi scheme. It was about three years after the accident when I started getting better that I noticed we were in big trouble with our business. Then I learned that most of the property had either been sold, or equity loans had been taken out on them and the loan payments had not been made and the banks were foreclosing or had already foreclosed on other properties." Marie sounded distressed now.

"You don't have to talk about it if it's too stressful for you," Craig commented.

"No, that's okay. It is good for me to talk about it. So when I asked Frank about these serious problems, he would say, 'Don't worry about it. I'll take care of it.' But it was all a lie and the problems got worse. I had a beautiful home in Scottsdale that we lost. And finally the day came when Frank was arrested and then the nightmare of the trial and the newspaper stories. It was awful."

There was a pause in the conversation before Craig asked, "How does someone get sidetracked into doing evil behavior?"

In a solemn manner Marie said, "We are all capable of doing evil things. It is important that we practice a means of being happy that does not bring injury to others. All of the major religions try to teach this. A good way to begin to understand this is to look at the basic instincts of man."

" 'The land of the two bellies,' is what Standing Bear would call our experience on earth," Marie continued. "Basically that means that we have two strong appetites. One is for food and the other is for sex. If we want to follow a way of life that will bring us true happiness, it is important that we don't become over infatuated with these appetites. Sometimes we are contributing to evil behavior just because we are not being conscious of our decisions. We can easily believe that satisfying a basic instinct want is our human right and not care about how our choice can hurt others."

"Isn't that being judgmental?" Craig asked.

"No. It is important that we have our preferences. We have to make choices all the time. It is best to make a choice that benefits all, not just you. If we are not careful about our choices, we could become out of balance, which is another word for 'dis-ease.' Sometimes this 'dis-ease' is physical and sometimes it is manifested in blatant evil behavior."

Craig nodded in agreement.

"One way to practice staying in balance is to include prayer and meditation in our daily habits." Marie was more upbeat now. "Our egos constantly can get us in trouble, because of their basic fear-driven outlook on life. By being prayerful and meditative, we can stop the ego chatter in our minds and become more peaceful and trusting in the higher awareness of the Creative

Spirit. In the realm of the Creative Spirit there is always abundance and safety."

"I've been practicing prayer and meditation for awhile now," Craig offered. "And I must agree that generally I feel more connected to my spirit self than I was before. However, sometimes it doesn't work for me."

"You need to trust the process. Remember that you have spirit guides that can help you with your anxious moments."

"Tell me again how I might know that a spirit guide is helping me."

"You need to develop your intuition. It is not as hard as you believe it might be. Begin by doing little things. For instance, when you ask for some little thing, like a parking space to open up and it happens, be immediately grateful and thank the spirit for helping you. As you become accustomed to asking for little favors in life and practice being instantly grateful for the results, you can move on to more advanced exercises."

Marie paused and looked intently at Craig for a moment. "Besides you are more connected to your spirit guide than you might believe. Remember when you were at NewStar and you went into the office and no one was there?"

"Yeah, sure." Craig had shivers going up his spine now.

"Why do you think that you weren't aware that there was a dead man on the other side?"

"Because I was out-of-touch with my intuition?"

"You could believe that, or you could believe that your spirit guides were offering a suggestive thought to your mind that everything was all right, so you would leave."

"What do you mean by that?" Craig was anxious now.

"I mean that if your intuition had been working for you like it normally would, and you would have been aware that something was wrong and you would have investigated and found the dead man, your behavior would have been entirely different."

"Yeah, I would have called the police."

"Exactly, and if you would have done that there is a chance that Frank would have come back and killed you too. Remember, he was watching the entire time. When you left right away in a calm manner, he probably assumed that you didn't notice anything unusual, and he could bide his time to injure you down the road in a more deliberate manner if he decided he needed to."

Craig shook his head trying to separate the anxious feeling he was having from his thoughts. "So the temporary lack of intuition actually protected me?"

"Exactly! In a reverse way your spirit guides were helping you."

"So, why don't I feel any better now; knowing that I have spirit guides that are helping me?"

Marie laughed. "You have to trust the process, Craig. At times it does feel awkward, because this is not the normal earth-way of doing things, and your ego becomes fearful when you consider that this is a way that could work for you. Trust me. Trust the process. It works." Marie smiled in a very caring way.

Carolyn had been quietly listening all this time, and then she slowly asked, "What is . . . the next thing we should do?"

"Craig, it is probably best if you go on with your work. When do you plan to go back to Minnesota?" Marie asked.

"My flight is scheduled to leave in two days."

"Good. That will give us some time to do something fun together."

"Let's take a trip to Sedona." Carolyn chimed in.

Going up to the high country of the red-rock-rimmed mountain mesas of Sedona was a good respite. The thin air was clean and crisp and the mood was calm. Once there, the trio sat on a mall veranda in Sedona and observed the beauty of the place. Getting away from the city helped them develop a sense of being in the "now" and they were enjoying the moment. While sitting in the sunlight in front of a shopping strip mall gathering energy from the sun, they seemed to transcend time and enjoyed the entrancing spell of Sedona.

It was fall and golden leaves were falling from the trees. Life's tempo seemed slower in the clear-aired mountain town. While white clouds floated across the blue sky, they soaked it all in. In front of a row of shops, there was a kaleidoscope of color among all the goods for sale. Noise from firecracker poppers and passing automobiles accented the air with a cacophony of sound. People walked by breaking the warm glow of the sun. Light was broken by moments of shadow. The tall, red-rocked walls standing back in the distance silently witnessed all this.

The atmosphere was perfect for continuing the conversation about the process of spiritual awareness.

"You know, I've come a long way since I first decided to try to change myself," Craig said. "I remember when I was full of negative thinking. I had a very low opinion of myself."

"Yes," Marie said. "I remember when you came to me for the first time. You were very sad."

"Thank God for you and others like you willing to help me," Craig continued. "I needed a lot of counseling and guidance because I had dug myself such a big hole of self-doubt, and self-denial. I remember at that time I had gone to a person named Shari, who had a studio here in Sedona."

"You have done good work," Marie said. "By believing in your power to heal yourself, you have set yourself up to succeed in changing."

"Recognizing that you want to change and having the belief in your ability to change is huge," Carolyn added.

"When we make the choice to heal ourselves, we are committing the most important part of healing. Healing the physical body works most effectively when we are committed to healing the emotional self. That is why you are physically healthier now, Craig, because you were courageous enough to do your emotional healing."

After enjoying a pleasant dinner at the Hideaway Restaurant, they drove back to Phoenix and once again stayed at Carolyn's house. The next morning Craig caught a plane back to Minnesota.

::::::

Frank arrived at the Flamingo Vallarta Hotel and Marina in the late evening. He liked this resort, because it is more like the old-styled Mexican hotel and marina. Although it had been only rated a 3-star hotel, it was close to the ocean and it had a lot of amenities.

The advertisement made it sound like it was better than it actually was:

At Flamingo Vallarta you will get the best of both Mexican traditional warmth and outstanding Mexican Pacific atmosphere. Have a pampering experience and let us treat you with comfortable accommodations and great facilities. Enjoy from the variety of our top quality specialties featured for your absolute palate's delight. Choose Mexican, International, or Italian delicious dishes at any of the two restaurants located throughout our hotel.

But, Frank didn't mind. At least here, the police would not be looking for him. He checked into his room and in no time was sound asleep.

CHAPTER FIVE

Return to Minnesota

I look for my lover in a sunrise through a dense fog.
Before dawn my heart yearns for intimacy.
As the haze becomes illuminated,
The beauty of the red orb and the enchanting light
Springs joy from my breast.
Visions of brighter light overcome my longings.
In that moment I only see the sunrise.

Craig had mixed feelings as he got off the plane at the Minneapolis –St. Paul Metropolitan Airport. In one way he was glad to be back in Minnesota, but another part of him missed the Arizona environment, the drama of the incident at NewStar, and being with Marie and Carolyn.

Back in the town of Flat Prairie, Craig felt alone. It had been about seven years since he had left Roseanne, his wife of 24 years. He arrived home alone, and for a long time sat and thought about all the change he had been through.

When Craig reported to work at the Safe 'n Sound headquarters in Flat Prairie the next day, he wasn't prepared for the greeting that he was given.

"Craig, good to see you," his boss, Bob Meyer, greeted him. "We heard you had some adventures in Phoenix."

"Yeah, there were more surprises than I bargained for," Craig responded.

"Well, here's another surprise," Bob Meyer said. "We've developed an improved chip for our security devices. These new chips will allow for more memory, so a longer period can occur to check back and playback an event. We've decided this improvement should be installed on all devices that we have installed in the last year, so we want you to go back and install those devices on all our equipment in Arizona and parts of Mexico. It will probably take you two weeks or so. When can you be prepared to go?"

"I just got back!" Craig exclaimed. "Can I have a little time to readjust?"

"How much time do you need? One day? Two days?"

Craig could tell Bob was anxious. He was a hard-working, six-foot, blonde-hair, balding Minnesotan of German descent. He had helped build this company to over 50,000 customers in ten states and had been quick to adopt innovative and leading-edge equipment. Craig had learned not to be surprised when something new would come up, because that was the norm at Safe 'n Sound. Also, he didn't really mind going back on the road. It was lonely for him living alone in Flat Prairie.

"Yeah, give me a couple days. Besides, I could use a little time to catch up on messages and errands back here before I go back."

"Okay. We're already preparing to send the equipment to your hotel in Scottsdale," Bob answered.

"Uh, if you don't mind, could we pick a different place?" Craig asked anxiously.

Bob paused, frowned, looked at Craig and finally said, "Okay. I bet that has something to do with the shooting at NewStar. Well, I'm not going to question you. If that is what you want, we can arrange that. Do you have any place in mind?"

"How about the Camelback Inn? They might have a discount this time of year."

"We'll check it out."

During the day, Craig decided to stop in at the Sun Rise Café in downtown Flat Prairie and get the latest news. The regular patrons were all seated in their usual places in the café. At one table a middle-aged farmer was talking about how his cousin had a friend who forgot where he parked his car at the Mall of America and it took two days to find it. Another not-to-be-out-done fellow mentioned that he had heard a friend of a friend had lost his car in an airport park and ride and it had taken three days to find it.

Craig saw his old friend and neighbor, T.T., sitting in the café. T.T. was a good spirited fellow who did a lot of fidgeting. He liked to say that he was graduated before they knew about attention deficit disorder.

"They used to ask me to self-diagnose myself. They'd ask me, 'What's wrong with you?' and I'd answer, 'I don't know.' Then they'd say, 'Then go sit in the corner until you figure it out.'"

He sat next to T.T., and said, "How's it going?"

"Not bad. Looks like it's going to rain tomorrow."

"It seems late in the season to be getting rain."

"Yeah, sure. Snow this time of year would be a good thing. But with this mostly cloudy sky from the volcanic activity going on, we probably won't have a normal winter."

"Probably not in a normal way."

"Probably not."

After Craig spent the day at work, he drove by the farm outside of town before returning to his small apartment in town. He remembered how excited they were when he and Roseanne found this five-acre place next to a large woods and small lake. Although the property was not bordering the woods or the lake, they could see both from their place, and that was good.

Upon returning home, he spent the better part of the evening preparing to leave his place again for two weeks and talking to his children on the phone.

Craig had two sons and one daughter. The youngest son, Tim, was only thirteen when Craig divorced Roseanne and he felt bad that he wasn't around him more when he was in high school. Now Tim was grown up and working for a medical device company in Minneapolis. His other son, Dan, worked in construction with an electrical contractor in St. James.

CHAPTER SIX

A Mexican Side Trip

Craig had to wait at the Minneapolis International Airport for almost four hours because of a flight delay. He hung around the food bazaars and ate in the large food court with the large glass-walled window looking out onto the west tarmac where planes dock to load & unload. At D'Amico & Sons, a fast food Italian restaurant, he got a cup of coffee.

Then he browsed in the stores - Travel Movie, Land's End, The Shoe Store, The Discovery Store, a bookstore, and the Minnesota Store where he bought a box of Burnsville Chocolates and some wild rice quick and creamy soup-base dry mix. The store had an interesting display of Minnesota items including loon knick knacks and wood carvings.

Finally, he waited in the pub by Gate 14, where old black and white pictures have been blown up to make wall murals. The mural that covered the north wall included a scene from the 1940s of six people boarding an airplane. The airplane is a large single-engine prop. A map alongside the mural shows Northwest Airlines flights to Rochester, Chicago, Milwaukee, La Crosse, Fargo, and Sioux Falls. There were about 16 people in the pub, all but two of them men. He sat by a couple who were speaking an interesting language that he didn't understand or recognize.

Craig had a beer and thought about how much his life had improved since he made several decisions to change. He was excited about another trip to Arizona and felt good about it.

He finally boarded flight #107 to Phoenix. It was a long boarding. It was raining out and the flight was delayed because of a problem loading the baggage.

After a three-hour-and-nine-minute flight, he arrived at Phoenix International Airport. From there, Craig caught a shuttle to the Camelback Inn where he rested until early the next morning. He then caught a cab to a Ramada Inn on Scottsdale Boulevard where he rented a car to drive to Mexico.

It was a whirlwind trip across the desert to Puerto Penasco Pinacante (Port of Rocky Point), which is located on the northern coast of the Gulf of California. Moving across the desert valley south of Gila Bend, Arizona, Highway 85 cuts through a vast landscape that is punctuated by mountains of rock that appear to have been pushed up out of the surrounding flat countryside. This area is largely uninhabited by people. Short trees grow out of rocky earth along dry washes, which clearly tell of water rushing across their beds; but the water cannot be seen. It is easy to imagine that the desert carries many other secrets besides where the water is hidden.

In the country along the U.S. Mexican border south of Ajo, Arizona into Oaxaca, Mexico, there is a large forest reserve. Cholla cactus, Palo Verde trees, and other vegetation seem to have been spaced apart with equal distance between them, and cragged rock peaks rise up to accent the sky. This creates an ethereal space. The author Castaneda described the southwestern desert landscape as being capable of causing our minds to imagine out-of-this-world realities. It is a place for visions. Along the journey through the desert, Craig stopped and walked away from the highway. He looked back and the highway had become a thin sliver. The vastness of the desert wilderness engulfed his immediate moment awareness. He sat there for a while and enjoyed a meditative moment.

When crossing the sandy desert country south of the beautiful forest reserve much of the time is spent approaching, going by, or leaving behind a large mountain range that looks like the Atlas Mountains of Northern Africa. Then the frequency of buildings and litter along the highway increases until the town of Puerto Penasco and the Sea of Cortez marks the highway's end.

Puerto Penasco is a fishing village that has become very popular with tourists, mostly from Phoenix; they call themselves Phoenicians. At night the stars are brilliant and the ocean smells and sounds create a magical quality. Craig checked into the

Hotel Las Glorias at 13 Armada Nacional Avenue located on the bay by the harbor where many fishing boats dock. In the bay, dolphins could be seen at play.

There are regularly scheduled boat trips that take people diving with the seals at Bird Island and also opportunities to go whale watching. The less adventurous go shopping at the outdoor malls. Alongside the bay, friendly merchants display their beautiful wares and entice shoppers to spend.

The Safe N' Sound customers included three resorts and Craig called all of them from the hotel telephone and made arrangements to make the needed installations. One of them was willing to let him come that afternoon. Soon he was back in his car and driving over to the Margaritaville Resort. After about two hours work, he was done. It was late afternoon and Craig was hungry, so he drove over to Old Town.

The Friendly Dolphin Restaurant at 44 Alcantar Avenue is located at the crossroads of Alcantar Avenue and Benito Juarez Boulevard. It is a popular restaurant and Craig parked a couple blocks away on Alcantar and walked back.

::::::

Frank decided a few days in Puerto Vallarta were long enough. He had business in Phoenix that he wanted to finish, so he was glad to catch a free ride to Puerto Penasco on the airplane of Senor Adimos Herangue, a businessman he had befriended in the few days he had spent in Mexico. Senor Herangue traveled between the two cities frequently and was doing very well as a trader of exotic art objects. He had several shops in both cities and was glad to give his new friend, Frank Gray, a ride to Puerto Penasco. Frank planned on taking a shuttle ride back to Phoenix and had only planned on being there a short while.

They were staying at the hacienda of Senor Herangue, and had only been in town about 24 hours when they decided to go out to eat in the Old Town section of Puerto Penasco. While they were driving down Benito Juarez Boulevard, Frank noticed Craig walking along the sidewalk.

'That's him,' Frank thought to himself. 'That's the guy from the NewStar building!'

::::::

Craig thought he heard someone say, "That's him, that's the guy from the NewStar building." He looked around but saw no one he recognized nor anyone paying any attention to him, and he thought, 'That's odd.' Then he walked up to the front door of The Friendly Dolphin.

::::::

Frank began obsessing on the opportunity he would have to eliminate the man from NewStar. He didn't want to create any suspicion from his acquaintance, Senor Herangue, so he thought he would only do something if the opportunity presented itself. They went to eat at The Point Restaurant, which was off of Malecon Kino Street.

Although the sun had set, it was early evening when they had finished eating and Senor Herangue decided he wanted to check on a couple of his shops in that area. He asked Frank if he minded just hanging around the promenade for a while. Frank was glad to oblige and was doing just that, when he decided to take a walk over to Benito Juarez Boulevard and the Friendly Dolphin.

As Craig walked out of the Friendly Dolphin, Frank was just across the street walking towards him. Craig turned to walk down Alcantar Street and was quickly out of Frank's view. Frank quickly jumped out into the street to cross over to Alcantar when a Toyota Prius driving fast down Benito Juarez Boulevard came up silently behind Frank. Frank only heard a slight noise and didn't have time to turn and look before the Prius smashed into his legs and sent him slamming down onto the cobbled street. He could feel the weight of the car under the wheel that drove over his left leg, back and head; and then he was unconscious.

Craig could see the commotion on the street when he drove up to Benito Juarez Boulevard to make the left turn to exit the Old Town area. 'Looks like someone had an accident,' he thought to himself as he turned onto the boulevard and drove away.

CHAPTER SEVEN
Earthquake

Waves lapping the shore
Pushed by a northerly wind
Pile foam onto the shore

The weather was cold and cloudy ever since Craig arrived in Phoenix. The result of volcanic activity in Oregon and Asia was the reason given for the strange weather. The massive amount of ash that was blown into the atmosphere was discussed and this heavy clouded weather had been predicted for some time. Now that it was happening, the weather patterns were disrupted and the sun was rarely seen. It was cloudy and raining almost constantly for the entire week.

Craig met Standing Bear by the Borgata Shopping Plaza in front of Trader Joe's.

"Hrmm. I'm glad you have some time to go up to Payson to visit us," Standing Bear flashed a brief grin. "Marie has been busy and hasn't been able to come to the city for over a week, so she was hoping you would come up there to visit."

Craig relished the idea of getting away to the Mogollan Rim country for the weekend. He had been busy installing the software updates and the work was so monotonous. He was in desperate need of a break.

As they drove north on Scottsdale Boulevard, the earth started undulating and rolling like the ocean seas. Everything started shaking. It seemed like it lasted for a long time. There was a fleeting moment when they didn't think they would make it out of that experience alive.

When the earthquake finally stopped, Craig and Standing Bear noticed people were staring with disbelief and fear.

As they looked around they observed some signs of destruction from the earthquake, such as cracks in the pavement and places where the pavement was uneven.

"Wow, was that ever scary!" Craig exclaimed while looking at Standing Bear.

Standing Bear had a very serious look on his face as he looked at Craig. "I wonder how big an area this earthquake is affecting?"

Craig didn't answer. He was feeling a sickness in his gut. He felt paralyzed and thought he should check his cell phone to see if there were any messages.

Meanwhile, Standing Bear decided to start driving again. There were a lot of cars that weren't moving. Some were damaged and others had run into each other. To get around them, Standing Bear was able to drive over the curb and over a crack in the sidewalk that was about eight inches wide and nine inches off level.

"I'm surprised your old truck is one of the few vehicles still running."

"Hrmm. It is old reliable, isn't it?"

"Yeah, you got a point there. What about the radio? Is there a reason it's not working?"

"It's broke."

"Do you think we should continue on this trip to Payson?"

"Hrmm. I don't want to stay in the city when it's this messed up."

They continued along and turned onto Shea Boulevard and out to Highway 87. The traffic was becoming more congested as other people were also trying to leave the city. There was a tremor about every fifteen minutes or so. It was upsetting to keep feeling the tremors.

"Wow, that was a big one," Craig said.

"Maybe you should call someone on your cell phone, and see if there is any news we should know about."

"I'll call Marie." Craig tried using his cell phone, but all he could get was static.

As they made their way out of town, it started to rain hard. When they got to the Tonto Basin north of Rye, the highway was damaged so much from the earthquake that no one could drive across the crack. There were a few cars on the south side of the crack and one on the north side. It was still raining, and Standing Bear and Craig could see people sitting inside the cars.

Standing Bear said, "I'll go take a look at the damage and talk to these people. There's no sense both of us getting wet, so you can sit here if you want."

"Okay, I'll sit here for awhile."

Standing Bear walked over to the crevasse and saw that it was about three feet wide and very deep. He looked down both directions of the crevasse to see if there was a place where the crevasse was closed up, but could see no other possibilities. Then he walked over to one of the parked cars, and the occupant rolled down her window.

"What do you think I . . . *we* . . . should do?" she asked.

"Hrmm. I don't know what to think," Standing Bear answered. "We need to decide to either turn around or look for another way. I don't want to sit here for very long."

"I don't know what to do. My car stopped a while ago and I haven't been able to get it started again. I wore down the battery trying to start it and now it is dead." She had a pitiful sound to her voice as she described her problem.

"Hrmm. I could give you a jump, but let's wait until we decide what we should do," Standing Bear answered warmly.

"Oh, thanks. By the way, my name is Sally," the lady answered.

"Standing Bear."

"Hi!"

"Hrmm. I'm going to go talk to my partner now, and I will get back to you."

"I . . . I'll be here, waiting."

Standing Bear walked over to his pickup and got in. "Hrmm. There's a major crevasse up there and I don't see where we can get across it."

"Do you have any ideas about what we should do?" Craig asked.

"Yes, let's pray and meditate for a moment, and a positive suggestion should come into mind."

Craig nodded, and the two of them went into a trance-like state, which only seemed like a moment to them, but actually lasted over 30 minutes. Rain fell the whole time. At one point Sally got out of her car and came walking over to the truck, but when she looked in, it looked like the two men were sleeping. "How odd," she thought to herself and walked back to her car.

Finally, Standing Bear came out of the trance and said, "There's a place about two hundred yards east of here where the crevasse comes together and we can cross, but only a pickup truck or a four-wheel drive vehicle will be able to make it."

"Can we go in this rain?"

"The rain will let up shortly, and we can go then."

::::::

Al Mencini was very anxious about all the news of severe weather changes being predicted because of all the volcanic activity. This meant he would have to gamble on where to acquire a comfortable estate, because his presence in Paradise Valley had become too uncomfortable. He was most distressed about the earthquake and what it had done to disrupt communications. He thought it was ominous that he had numerous problems trying to communicate with people the other day also, and a wire transfer for a large sum of money from his Phoenix bank to a bank in the Cayman Islands had been disrupted. It took several days to finally get that mess straightened out. Meanwhile, the FBI had called and they were investigating the large money transfer. This made him very nervous, and he had planned to immigrate to the Cayman Islands soon to avoid just such a confrontation.

Mencini had helped drug smugglers and dealers launder their money for over 12 years. He had also been an informant for the CIA and had helped them with a government overthrow in Latin America. His involvement with Frank Gray and that Ponzi scheme continued to be a nagging problem for him. However, when Frank Gray was indicted and convicted, Mencini had never been part of the inquiry. He was clever in his ability to stay distant from the criminals that he aided. However, he had been investigated before the Ponzi scheme because of his involvement with Frank Gray. The FBI had not been able to discover any hard evidence, no paper trail, and nothing could be proven. Mencini had asked the CIA if they could help and that resulted in some accidental disappearance of records.

This latest snafu with the money transfer renewed suspicions with the FBI. There was a chance that now the government might have the information that they needed to implicate Mencini with the Ponzi scheme or some other wrong doings.

Frank Gray had been loyal to him and had not implicated him in anyway and for that he was grateful. Nevertheless, the FBI investigators had discovered that Al Mencini was connected with some of the money that had changed hands with Frank Gray. He had been implicated and indicted by the prosecuting attorney, but no solid evidence was ever proven. When he learned that Beamquist was willing to testify about the connection between Gray and himself, he knew he had to silence Beamquist. He was grateful that Gray had been willing to do that, but he was also anxious about Gray's ability to function discretely. Al was not pleased to have learned that Frank had left Puerto Vallarta, and he didn't know where he was.

The earthquake had Mencini "shook up," and all the flights in and out of the Phoenix airport were canceled. Mencini immediately packed his bags and made a decision to go north to Flagstaff or Vegas where he could catch a flight from there. He packed about $300,000 in cash, which he cleverly hid inside of hollowed out books. He wanted to be prepared for anything, and he planned this getaway. He decided that he should get away soon, because the FBI would be looking for him. All the hassle and confusion that would come with the aftermath of this earth-quake would surely have the FBI in a flux also. So he summoned his chauffeur and body guard, Max Coupley, who was a balding six-foot-two, two hundred and thirty pound man. Max had worked for him for over twenty years and was very loyal.

They got into Mencini's Lexus and headed up towards Payson. There were a lot of cars stopped on the streets and as they trav-eled along there were others that were also moving. In order to get around some of the stopped cars, they had to drive along the shoulder or on sidewalks. It took them at least an extra hour to get outside of town and onto Highway 87. The frequent tremors added even more anxiety to the trip.

They got as far as the Tonto Basin north of Rye when they came upon a group of cars stopped in the middle of the road.

::::::

While Standing Bear and Craig were still sitting in the Ford pickup truck, another vehicle pulled up behind them. Soon a large fellow got out from the driver's side and walked up to Standing Bear's window.

"Does anybody know what's going on here?" Max asked in his deep, bass voice.

"Yeah, there's a major rift in the road and there's no way any of us can get across it."

"What do you plan to do?"

"We're going to wait until the rain lets up and then we're going to go off-road and look for a place to cross east of here."

"Oh," Max answered and then walked back to the Lexus.

Max told Mencini what he had learned. Mencini thought briefly and cursed a lot. Finally, he decided, "Max, see if those people can give me a ride to Payson, or even Flagstaff if they are going that far. Maybe I can buy a ride in Payson, if I have to, to get to Flagstaff. I don't want to leave the Lexus here, so if they say yes, than you can take the car back to Phoenix. Only you won't go to my place, but to your place. If the cops ask you any questions, you can say I am in Mexico until the weather changes."

"Yes boss. I'll see if they will give you a ride."

Max got out and walked over to the pickup again. When Standing Bear rolled down his window, Max asked him, "Any chance you fellows might give my boss a ride to Payson or Flagstaff? I'll take his car back to Phoenix, but he really wants to go to the airport at Flagstaff."

Craig could feel a sensation on the back of his neck. He was getting a major warning signal. 'Why am I reacting like this?' he thought.

Standing Bear turned away from Max and looked toward Craig. "What do you think?"

"Uh, I guess so. Bringing him to Payson should work out."

"Alright, I'll go tell him." Max walked away.

"I don't know why, but I have a funny feeling about this." Craig looked at Standing Bear.

"Once we get across the rift, it should only be a few minutes and we'll be in Payson."

"Yeah, you're right. It's no big deal."

Soon, Max was back with Mencini's luggage. Standing Bear got out again and stuffed the luggage under the tarp that was covering the other gear in the back. Then Standing Bear walked over to Sally's car to talk to her.

"Hrmm. As soon as it stops raining, we are going to go off-road to the east and look for a place to cross the rift. I don't think your car will be able to do that, but we will get you started and maybe you should go back where you came from."

"Okay," Sally answered. I'll be right here waiting." She smiled calmly.

A moment later, Mencini was climbing into the cab of the pickup with Craig and Standing Bear.

"Hi," he introduced himself. "My name's Al.

"Craig."

"Standing Bear."

"Thanks for the ride."

"No problem. We're going through Payson, anyway."

Max turned around with the Lexus and headed back to Phoenix. Then the rain let up.

Standing Bear started the pickup truck and drove alongside the car Sally was in. "Hrmm. This shouldn't take long," he said as he got out of the truck and walked over to Sally. "Pop your hood."

Sally nodded her head and reached down to grab the lever that would open her hood. Once the hood popped open, Standing Bear walked around to the front of her car and opened it up all the way. While he was doing this, Craig got out and offered to assist. Standing Bear grabbed his jumper cables from under his tarp and said, "Put the red cable on the positive side of the battery."

Craig did that to Sally's car while Standing Bear hooked up his pickup truck. He told Sally, "We'll wait a few minutes for the battery to get charged up some, before we try to start your car."

Sally cleared her throat. "Oh . . . okay," she said. "And thanks again for the help."

After a few minutes, Craig gave Sally the signal to start, and her car started.

As they put away the cables and closed the engine hoods, they said their goodbyes and Sally turned around and headed back towards Phoenix while the rusty red pickup truck bounced off the road into the high-desert country following the rift east.

After a few minutes they came to a place where it looked safe to cross, so they crossed to the other side. Then they headed back to the highway.

A couple SUVs that had been sitting on the opposite side of the crevasse started driving across the desert towards them when they saw that they had safely crossed the crevasse. There were four cars that were still on the highway and the drivers were gathered in a group. When the pickup got back to the highway, they stopped to talk to the people.

"What a predicament," the shrill-voiced spokeswoman for the group said to Standing Bear. "We've got people that insist they have to get to Phoenix. Another car won't start, because the batteries are dead, and we're trying to sort it out." She was an elderly lady with a lot of spunk.

"Well, I can help the car get started," Standing Bear said. "And then we're going to Payson."

"All right. Good."

Meanwhile, two people in the group wanted to leave their cars alongside the road and catch a ride to Phoenix with the two SUVs that had arrived on the other side of the crevasse and stopped to talk across the crevasse. A rope was tossed across the crevasse and tied to the bumper of a vehicle on both sides, and the people jumped across with one hand on the rope for safety.

Finally, the pickup truck was on its way to Payson. After arriving in Payson, they went to a car dealer, that had a car rental sign up, and they pulled into the lot. Mencini got out.

"Go in and see if you can get a rental car. We'll wait here," Standing Bear offered.

"Thanks, gentlemen," Mencini said as he got out and walked into the car dealer showroom.

After a bit, Mencini came out with news. "The earthquakes have damaged the electrical grid and also a lot of the roads are blocked off because of damage to them. Also, because of the disaster, access to cell phones has been blocked, so emergency crews can use their cell phones and radios without interruption. As a result, the dealers in this town won't let any more of their cars go out. They have many of their cars out now, and the mechanics are besides themselves trying to fix the problems with the ones in the shop, because they don't have any electricity. Also, there have been widespread earthquakes and the lower

Colorado River and Gila River are flooding, including the city of Yuma."

"Wow!" Craig exclaimed. "This is a major disaster. What should we do with you, Al? Do you want a ride to a motel to wait this out?"

"Yeah, I guess so. I'll find a place to lay over until things settle down." Al started thinking that he did not want to spend a couple days in Payson. Besides, if the FBI was looking for him, hanging out in a place like Payson wouldn't be smart."

"I'm going to go back in and talk to these guys one more time. Please wait a moment for me," Mencini said. And when Standing Bear nodded his head, he turned and walked back into the dealership. He asked if he could use the telephone, since his cell phone didn't work. He wanted to call the airport and see about getting an air plane ride. They let him do that, and he learned that there was a plane leaving soon, but it was already full. He would have better luck in Flagstaff. Then he went into the bathroom and checked his gun to make sure it was loaded.

Meanwhile outside, Craig and Standing Bear were waiting.

"I don't know about this guy," Craig said. "He gives me the willies."

"Hrmm. I agree," Standing Bear said. "I could hear him think about avoiding the FBI. Now why would anyone have to avoid the FBI?"

"You could hear him think?" Craig made a twisted look with his face. "Where is that coming from?"

"Hrmm. Just listen to the notions that come into your thoughts." Standing Bear was looking very seriously at Craig now. "If something sounds like something someone else would say, it probably is someone else, and you're picking it up through mental telepathy." Then, without speaking, he added, "You dummy."

"Don't call me a dummy!" Craig responded.

Standing Bear looked at him with a big grin on his face. "Say what?"

And they both laughed.

They were still laughing when Mencini came out of the dealership and got into the truck. Standing Bear returned to the street and continued driving along Route 87. He was getting ready to turn off Highway 87 and into a Best Western Hotel parking lot, when Mencini pulled out his 9 millimeter pistol.

"I want you to keep driving on this highway," he said in a low, mean voice.

"Yes sir," Standing Bear said as he continued down the road.

When they got to the north edge of town, Mencini said "Pull over here."

Standing Bear pulled onto the shoulder of the road.

"Now get out!" Standing Bear opened the door and began getting out when Mencini poked Craig and said, "Both of you!" Then Craig slid over and got out too.

Mencini was sliding right behind Craig and when Craig's feet touched the ground, Mencini was already in the driver's seat. A moment later, he had the truck in gear and was pulling away.

Standing Bear and Craig stood alongside the highway looking at each other and then at the pickup truck quickly moving away.

"I told you something was funny about him," Craig said angrily. He was very upset about not listening to his gut feelings and thus being stranded along the highway.

"Hrmm," Standing Bear grunted.

"What do we do now?"

"Walk." And they started walking along the highway.

After about a mile, Standing Bear started heading into the driveway of a small ranch.

"What are you thinking?" Craig said.

"Maybe we can borrow a couple horses here."

"I like the way you think," Craig said.

They walked up to the front door of the house just about the time another tremor came.

CHAPTER EIGHT
Another Way of Traveling

Along the roadway
A yellow beaked blackbird
Struts and looks about.

Charley Norman was an older fellow with a hunchback. He made a snorkeling sound when he laughed and he had a slight limp. Once a cowboy in his younger years, he had suffered multiple injuries from working on a large ranch in the Verde Valley. His own ranch wasn't very big, but it had enough room to board a few horses during the wet years. He currently had about a dozen of them.

"Who's that?" he yelled, when Standing Bear knocked on his front door.

"Standing Bear."

There was a moment of silence, then the sounds of shuffling right before the door opened. A shorter fellow peered at them through a screened door.

"What the hell are you guys doing out during this hellish time?" he barked.

"Hrmm. We were trying to get up to Marie's when we had our pickup truck stolen," Standing Bear said with no emotion in his voice.

Charley made his strange snorkeled laugh. "Why that's the most pathetic news I've heard all day, and there has been a lot of bad news today! Come in, come in," he said as he opened the door all the way and stepped sideways.

Standing Bear got right to the point. "We're wondering if you would lend us a couple horses and tack. Also, I'd like to call the Highway Patrol and report my stolen truck."

Charley watched Standing Bear as he talked and then he looked down and in a quiet voice said, "I guess that'd be all right." Then looking back up at both Craig and Standing Bear, he asked, "How long you thinking?"

"Hrmm. It will be overnight for sure, and probably longer." Standing Bear shifted the weight on his feet.

There was another tremor.

"Jesus, watch how you shift your weight Standing Bear," Charley said in a serious manner with a smile on his face. Then, "Well, there's the phone." And turning to Craig, "Let's go out to the barn and get you fellows set up."

A gelding paint and a bay mare were both ponies in good riding form and it was on them that Craig and Standing Bear rode out onto Highway 87. Charley outfitted them with feedbags and oats too, so the horses would have extra feed for the workout they were probably going to get.

It was now dusk. They only had ridden about two miles when they came upon a vehicle that had gone off the road and had hit a large boulder. It was obvious that the passengers needed help, so they stopped to help them. There was a young woman and her eight-year-old boy. The woman was bleeding and the boy was crying. Standing Bear was able to devise a dressing for the woman's wounds from a white cotton shirt that the lady had. After talking with them for a while, they learned that the woman had been able to call her husband in Verde, who was coming to get them.

Finally, the duo was on their way again. They got within two miles of Marie's place when night fell completely dark. They had to stop because they could not see where to go. There was no other traffic and no electric lights were shining anywhere. They stopped when they could tell by the sounds of the horses hoofs that they were off the road.

"Hrmm. I hope the clouds pass over," Standing Bear said. "Until they do, we have to stay here."

So they dismounted and tied the reins of their mounts to their wrists and they lay down on the ground. Craig was exhausted and soon was sound asleep. Slowly he noticed that he was looking down on himself and Standing Bear sleeping with their two horses standing over them. He was also thinking about what Phoenix looked like and his spirit rose up into the sky and instantly he was over Phoenix. From there he could see much devastation. The only lights were those of vehicles driving around and areas where there were search and rescue operations going on. The amount of damage to the area was extensive. This realization struck a chord of fear into Craig, and instantly he was back in his body. In that moment he was content to be in his body and he slept some more without dreaming.

Suddenly, Standing Bear was shaking him. "Get up. Let's go."

Craig slowly woke up and, looking above him, he could see a brilliant star-studded sky.

"The clouds have moved away and we have enough light to travel now. Let's go. We only have a little further to go."

Standing Bear started mounting his horse when he saw Craig stand up. Craig also mounted his horse, and they were soon riding through the night. And so it was that they finally arrived at Marie's about midnight. They found a place to tie up the horses and they took off the saddles and bridles before going into the house.

"Oh, it's so good to see you guys. We were so worried," Marie greeted them enthusiastically.

"If it wasn't for the earthquake and robbery, we would have been here sooner," Craig said.

"What robbery?"

"We gave a fellow a ride and he ended up pulling a gun on us and taking the truck."

"Oh, that explains the call from the highway patrol. They called to let us know they found your truck by Mormon Lake."

"Hrmm. Mormon Lake? He was going to the airport in Flagstaff. Maybe he ran out of gas," Standing Bear thought out loud.

"Well, you guys must be exhausted. Let's go to sleep and talk more in the morning."

It was close to 9 o'clock when Craig finally got up and started moving around. No one was in the house. He looked out the window and could see purple colored mountains in the distance. There were birds flying and the smell of the mountain air still had the fresh smell of morning. He walked into the kitchen and could see the remains of a hearty breakfast and suddenly he remembered how hungry he was. He grabbed a piece of bread and started eating. There was a cold egg and juice and he turned on the stove to warm up water for a hot tea. While he was enjoying his breakfast, Marie and Carolyn came walking in.

"It looks like sleeping beauty finally decided to get up!" they chided.

"I was sleeping so hard that I never heard anything. There must have been some commotion to make all this great-tasting food this morning." Craig took a drink of his glass of juice.

"It sounds like you guys had an event-filled day yesterday," Carolyn said in her slow-paced voice.

"Yes. The chaos from this earthquake has really messed things up."

"Have you heard the latest news?" Carolyn offered.

"No. What can you tell me?" Craig asked.

"To begin, Phoenix and the lower valley had several big earthquakes yesterday. The crevasses from the earthquakes are so wide by Yuma that the ocean has backed up and completely flooded Yuma. In California there also are vast areas of Los Angeles and the Bay area that have been swallowed up by the ocean. The Roosevelt Dam has been badly damaged and the authorities are afraid that the dam might break and cause major flooding in Mesa, Tempe and lower Phoenix. To add to the confusion there are fires burning all over Sun Valley."

Craig remembered his dream experience last night and he shuddered. "There must be a lot of people suffering."

"Oh, that's not the half of it. There also were more volcanic eruptions in northern California and Washington, and steam explosions where the oceans have swept into the earthquake cracks. This is expected to cause more disruption to the weather patterns. Presently our weather is coming from Mexico, which is receiving rain from the Pacific Ocean. We can expect more cloudy rainy weather."

"And someone has to go with Standing Bear to get his truck," Marie said with her right hand on her right hip, determined to get the conversation off of the weather.

"I'd be willing to ride with Standing Bear again," Craig said. He had grown very fond of this big Indian, who had a lot of wisdom and very healing ways.

"There's more going on than just stolen trucks." Marie was very serious now. "There's also the problem of the Sedona vortex."

'The Sedona vortex?' Craig thought to himself.

"Yes, the Sedona vortex is a major earth energy center for this region," Marie continued. "In the 1920s Sedona was an artists community. In those days there were a number of very knowledgeable light-energy workers around, who had done their ley line assessment of that area and found a hierarchy between the vortexes in that region. The major vortex was the vortex of the sphinx. But they also found out that when they held a ruby in that area, all of the other vortexes in that region would start to vibrate the same way and with the same frequency. From their aesthetic knowledge they deduced that was a wonderfully good thing, so one of them commissioned Frank Lloyd Wright to build the chapel by the sphinx vortex. Within that chapel was a place to set the ruby stone. Unfortunately, after several decades, the meaning for the placement of the ruby was lost on those who manage the place. One day the ruby was discovered and carelessly moved to a museum in central Sedona."

"What are ley lines?"

"The ley lines and their intersection points are believed by some to resonate a special psychic or mystical energy, often including elements such as geomancy. It is believed that points on lines have electrical or magnetic forces associated with them."

"Who were the bygone light-energy workers?"

"Those light workers have been rumored to be from the Hermetic Order of the Golden Dawn, which was a group that studied ancient ways and practiced spiritual development. It is believe that group was started by the Freemasons, which is the same group that George Washington, Thomas Jefferson, and John Adams were members of."

"So, what's the problem with the vortex?"

"There are still some knowledgeable healers around, who believe that if the ruby is returned to its original resting place, this area will suffer less destruction from these earth-changing events."

"So, why don't they just put the ruby back?"

"It gets complicated," Marie sighed. "The keepers of the chapel would love to have the ruby returned, but the museum curator is not anxious to go along with that. We've arranged to have her release the ruby, if this document is given to her." Here Marie pulled an envelope out of her vest pocket.

Craig shuddered. He felt like he was out of his body as he heard Marie say, 'We want you to help bring this to Sedona and move the ruby stone pendant to its rightful resting place.' She was smiling. Carolyn was also looking at him and smiling a sweet demure smile.

"Shouldn't someone, who has the proper authority, be assigned to move the ruby stone?"

"Whoever holds this document will have the authority, and we want you to be that person."

Craig was stunned. He was surprised by this request and was hesitant, but it seemed so obvious to him what he had to do. "Okay I'll do it. Will Standing Bear be coming with me?"

"We've talked about that, and we hope you agree that it's important that Standing Bear bring the truck and its cargo back here."

"What is in the truck that you are so anxious to get?"

"We want to set up this site for helping people and to keep our communication channels open. We have a variety of equipment

and supplies in the back of Standing Bear's truck that we need."
Marie held Craig by both hands and looked directly into his eyes.
"Craig, you are a very strong and courageous person. Please
agree to do this. It will do so much good for so many people."

Craig was touched and he said, "Yes, of course. I already agreed.
I just want to know more of what's going on. I am disappointed
that Standing Bear won't be coming with me."

At this moment Standing Bear came walking into the room.
"We'll travel together as far as Mormon Lake, and I think you'll
like Amel here as a partner."

And there standing next to Standing Bear was a medium-built
dark-haired, light-skinned Indian, Amel Atnash. Amel was an
architect from England and his mother was from India. He had
worked for years in Chicago and only recently had moved to
Arizona. Another man stepped in and stood behind. He was also
medium-build and had light brunette hair, which was cut short.
His name was Jim Thoreau, and he was an electrical engineer
with strong mechanical experience.

Both of these fellows had known Marie from her visits to Phoenix.
They had been up in the Mogollan Rim country when the earthquake happened, and had decided to stop in at Marie's to see if
she was okay. It then became obvious to both of them that they
should stay and help with the relief effort at this place.

After Craig had been introduced to these people there was a
quick review of needed equipment and preparation for the next
journey. It had been decided to use horses wherever possible.
Most of the gasoline pumps weren't working because of the
failure of the electric grid. Many of the roads had been damaged
and it was not possible to discover where or predict when they
would be or would not be passable by a motorized vehicle. Also,
there were places in some roadways where so many cars had
been damaged and were blocking the roads such as on bridges
that the only predictably reliable way to travel was by horse.
They had already called Charley and got his permission to use
the horses for a few days.

CHAPTER NINE
The Sedona Chapel Challenge

Above the shining water,
A large bird glides
Shimmering in the early morning sun.

Most everything had been gathered and packed with Standing Bear's supervision. The plan was for all four men to travel by horseback to the top of the Mogollan Rim. There, Jim would walk over to the Peterson ranch at the top of the Verde Valley and get two more horses and equipment and then return to Marie's. The other three would continue on to Mormon Lake.

By the time they had started out on their journey it was late morning. Standing Bear was carrying gasoline in a bladder and extra water and the feed bags on one horse, and Craig and Amel rode the other horse. They followed Highway 87 through Strawberry and over the Mogollan Rim and into the Coconino Forests. There wasn't much traffic. Now and then they would meet or be passed by a car or pickup truck. By evening they were just north of Happy Jack where they found a place to camp and rest for the night.

After setting up their tents and starting a fire, the group sat around and talked. Standing Bear started the evening conversaton. "Hrmm. Have you noticed how much quicker results from manifesting thought have been occurring lately?"

"What are you talking about?"

"It seems to me that everything we want has been provided for us within moments of wanting it. When I wished for horses from Charley's place, that happened. When I wished for the police to find my truck, that happened. I don't know, but I'm feeling both fortunate and empowered by the way things manifest for us."

"It is important to be grateful for the small gifts in life, if the law of manifestation is going to work," Craig offered. "I know there have been a lot of wonderful things in my life that did not happen until I had a vision of what I wanted and then believed that they would be possible in my life. Some things happened so long after I had the vision of what I wanted that I momentarily forgot that I had wished for them to come to pass."

"I wanted to spend some time in the Cococino Forest, but this isn't exactly the way I wanted it," Amel said with a smile, and they all laughed.

"Hrmm. But don't you think that when you have a vision of what you want and you believe you can get what you want, that it will happen quickly?" Standing Bear was back on his original point.

"It depends what you want," Amel said. "I would like to have a hot bath, but that's not going to happened."

"Yes, it depends on what you want," Craig said. "I believe that if you are on your soul's true journey, than what you need to accomplish your goals can easily be acquired or come into your life."

"Exactly!" Standing Bear jumped in. "And I believe we are on our soul's journey now! Hrmm. We were all meant to be where we are now – helping make things better for the people while being in our integrity and following the ways of the earth."

Both Amel and Craig nodded and voiced their agreement.

"And also," Standing Bear continued, "It is important to stay out of the place of fear. Be courageous and know that there are many, who can help you. Unfortunately, when we are fearful, the tools of manifesting and communicating with each other through telepathy won't work for our benefit. In other words, if you are feeling fearful, that is what you will attract - fearful situations."

Here Standing Bear paused and the group was quiet because they could sense that Standing Bear was about to make another point. "As we set about to achieve our goals tomorrow, we may come into some difficulties. Hrmm. Don't be discouraged, and instead think about what you need to continue on your mission. In all likelihood something will appear or happen that will aid your mission."

"I hope I can be brave enough to stay calm if we get into a difficult situation," Amel said and Craig agreed.

"Well, here is something that might come in handy as you journey through the forest tomorrow," said Standing Bear as he handed Craig a nine-millimeter pistol.

"I hope I don't need to use that!" Craig exclaimed as he reached out to take it.

"Hrmm. I hope not either, but there are big cats and other creatures in the forest that could be an adversity. It's a just-in-case measure. I'm packing another one. Amel has already told me he won't use a gun, so I didn't give him one."

Amel nodded his head in agreement.

Craig said, "You're full of surprises Standing Bear." And he stuffed the pistol in his bag and prepared for sleep

"Better safe than sorry. Let's get a good night's sleep now. We're going to have another big day tomorrow."

In the morning they had a light breakfast and saddled up and headed for Mormon Lake. Along the way they were passed by a pickup truck with two fellows dressed in camouflaged clothing inside and a lot of gear in the back. They shouted a greeting as they passed.

At Mormon Lake the trio found the rusty red pickup truck. It was parked alongside the road and was out of gas. The back cargo box was still covered with tarp and inside was all the gear that they had hoped to recover. After they helped Standing Bear transfer the gasoline from the bladder into the truck and he had unloaded all the gear that the remaining duo would not need, Craig and Amel headed to the west side of the lake where they would discover a trail that would take them to Sedona.

Craig felt anxious about the trip as he left his stalwart companion, Standing Bear. He felt ominous about the journey to Sedona and he felt fearful and anxious because he had not been responding to his hunches like he could have to avoid trouble.

It was a well-marked road and could have been traveled with the truck, but traveling by horse suited Craig just find. However, his new partner, Amel, complained a lot about the ride.

"The inside of my legs are screaming at me," he started complaining not long after they left Mormon Lake. "We should stop and take a break."

"That won't help much, because it will just hurt that much more after we get back on the trail."

They traveled for a while and came across the pickup truck they had seen earlier parked alongside the trail with the occupants standing on the ground. They were watching them as they rode up and one of them said, "Howdy. Where are you guys going?"

"Sedona. Where did you guys come from? Have you come from Phoenix? Any news about what it's like in Phoenix?"

"Yeah. We left Phoenix this morning. It's a mess there. A lot of damage from the earthquakes and there are fires burning and the firemen can't get to them, or if they do, there's no water in the hydrants because of the damage to the water system. It's a mess, so we left this morning. My buddy, Jim here and I decided to come up to the forests and live off the land for a few days until things settle down a bit." The man had a blue and white bandana wrapped around his head. He was dressed in camouflage clothes.

Craig had a notion that something wasn't right about these guys and he urged his horse to move on. As the horse started walking he said, "Well, I hope that works out for you guys. Meanwhile people are expecting us in Sedona, so we're going to keep moving."

The fellow in the blue and white bandana quickly moved around in front of Craig's horse and blocked its way. The horse reared his head up as the man moved directly in front of it.

"Whoa there. We were just thinking what a fine couple of horses you all got." He now had a pistol pulled out.

Craig reined in his horse. Amel was behind and alongside Craig away from the armed man, so the man stepped backwards and into the edge of the treeline, so he could see them both. His friend was not as confident as the blue-bandana man as he stayed by the truck, but he also had a gun out now.

Craid was paralyzed with fear. A sinking feeling weighed in his gut. Then he thought of Standing Bear's words and suddenly, but not willfully, had a vision of a mountain lion or puma, as they are known in Arizona. He looked up and there in the pine tree on a big branch above the blue-bandana man was a big cat. Craig already had a look of fear on his face, and he wished the big cat would jump the man who threatened him. Surprising everybody in that moment, the big cat leaped down on the blue-bandana man.

"Aiyeee!" the man screamed as the big cat landed on him and the both of them went crashing to the ground. The second man had all his attention focused on his friend and the cat and pointed his gun at the struggle.

Meanwhile, Craig's horse reared up and, with very little urging, the two horses and their mounts went bounding down the trail and away from the highway robbers. They were high on adrenalin after that incident and, after running their horses for about a mile, they stopped galloping but continued to move quickly for three hours before stopping to rest at Pinewood. Then they followed Interstate 17 a few miles to the exit to Munds Mountain Wilderness area, which had a trail going towards Sedona.

Craig was sick to his stomach with fear and self-doubt after the encounter with the two highway robbers. When he and Amel stopped to rest, he let his fears be known.

"I don't know why I let myself get talked into doing this," he lamented. "It's bad enough having to have my life disrupted by this big earthquake, but riding a horse through a dangerous forest towards a destination for the purpose of moving a gemstone hardly seems like it's worth it."

But Amel was staying centered to his true self and said. "That was a scary encounter and we're lucky we escaped without any injury. I'm sick to my stomach from all this too. If it had been anybody else but Marie that had asked us to go, I probably wouldn't have come. I do not like riding horses. We just have to trust this process and be brave. Hopefully, it will all make sense later."

"Damn, I'll be glad when this is over," Craig added.

When they arrived above Sedona it was early evening and after sunset. They could see lights flashing and some traffic and other signs of activity in the community as they looked down from the rim vantage point. They decided to take the rim trail road down to Sedona and spend the night somewhere below before continuing on with their mission in the morning. By the time they were below the rim and in Sedona, it was night.

They had to dismount and walk toward the stream on the east side of Sedona as they brought their horses to get a much needed drink of water. They held the horses back after they had some water, for fear the horses would flounder themselves by overdrinking. Then, after taking the saddles off and standing with them for a few minutes, they brought the horses back to the stream and let them drink some more, before pulling them away a second time. Craig had to teach Amel to do this, because Amel wasn't aware of the problem a horse could make for himself if he was overly thirsty. Finally, the horses were satiated. They tied them up and after a while fed them.. The supply of oats was then gone.

The night sky was clear and the stars gave them some light. There were very few electrical lights coming from Sedona. Apparently the electrical grid was out here too, and the sound of small engines gave them the clue that several small electrical generators were providing the electrcity for the few lights scattered sporadically in the town.

Amel and Craig had to spend the night with their horses by the creek. They set up the one tent they had and tried to get comfortable, but the land they were on was rocky and uneven and it was difficult to find a position to rest. Eventually they passed out from exhaustion.

CHAPTER TEN

Hanging a Red Ruby

With jumping horses
And shaking earth and rocks,
The red stone is placed.

In the early light of dusk, they were awakened by the rumbling and shaking of a tremor. They were both stiff and sore. When they grumbled their way up and out of the tent, they were greeted by two badly shaken horses, who whineyed their fearful reaction to the tremor. They were pulling on their tethers as Craig and Amel stepped next to them and tried to calm them by speaking softly and stroking their necks. After the horses settled down, Craig and Amel broke camp, packed their gear, saddled their horses, and prepared to ride into town.

They were close to the bridge over Oak Creek, and they soon crossed it and were in an area of Sedona where a restaurant could be found. Craig and Amel were both hungry and thinking about a fine breakfast when they came upon a restaurant that looked like it was open. They tied their horses to the posts in front of the restaurant and walked in.

A middle-aged, overweight, brown-haired woman with glasses and a white apron looked at them as they walked in and asked, "You guys hungry?"

"Are we ever," they answered in unison.

"Well sit down and let me tell you what we got," she said with a friendly tone. As they sat down she began telling them, "I can cook you eggs and bacon, potatoes and onions, but we ain't got any bread. But I can make pancakes. There ain't been a bread truck or a milk delivery here since the earthquakes started."

"How about juice or coffee?" Amel asked.

"I can do coffee, but only have apple juice."

"That sounds great," Amel said.

"I'll have that and whatever you're cooking," Craig said. "Including the pancakes."

After they received their hot breakfast meal, and while they were eating, the cook and waitress talked to them.

"Where did you fellows ride from?"

"Mormon Lake."

"Why'd you come to Sedona?"

And Craig and Amel explained that they were on a mission to the Sedona Heritage Museum. They had to pick up something that was very important, and the persons who asked them wanted it as soon as possible.

"Sounds weird to me," the cook said before she gave the duo directions to the museum. "But in Sedona, a lot of stranger things happen."

Within 30 minutes they were at the museum. It was only a few minutes before nine o'clock.

The sign in front of the building read, 'Sedona Heritage Museum - 735 Jordan Road, Sedona. Open: daily - 11:00 to 16:00.'

It seemed like a strange place to come looking for a ruby stone. After all, it is a heritage museum that showcases the history of the city and region, including exhibits and movies that have been filmed in the area. The museum itself is sited on an old apple orchard and housed in a historic home, complete with period furnishings and antiques.

'I hope the curator is here,' Craig thought to himself as he grabbed the front door of the museum and opened it.

The door hit a bell hanging by a string from the ceiling as Craig and Al stepped into the old farmhouse. In a moment, a white-haired old lady came into the room. "We're not open yet," she exclaimed. Then, as she looked over the two scruffy looking characters, "I bet you're here for a different reason."

"Yes, we're here to pick up a ruby stone and bring it to the Wright Chapel of the Holy Cross by the Sphinx vortex," Craig said as he pulled out the envelope with the document giving him the authority.

The lady walked over to take the envelope from Craig. She looked intently at both Craig and Amel, then opened the envelope and peered at the paper that came out of it. After a moment she said, "It all appears to be in order." She walked back into the room she came out of and returned shortly with a small box that she gave to Craig.

"Thank you," Craig said as he took the box. He opened the box and inside was a beautiful cut ruby stone in a gold setting, which had a small eyelet on one end so it could be used as a necklace or a pendulum. Attached to the Ruby was a gold chain.

"It's beautiful," he said as he showed it to Amel.

"Yes," Amel said as he looked at it.

Then Craig closed up the box and put the jewel in his jacket pocket. "We'll now bring it over to the chapel. Thank you again for being open when we arrived," Craig said to the lady.

"Yes, that was fortunate. But I expected you to be arriving today, so I have been keeping an eye out for you. God speed," she said.

The duo stepped back outside and climbed on their horses and rode out.

It took another 30 minutes to get to the approach off of Highway 179 to the Chapel of the Holy Cross by the Sphinx. About the time they started up the street off of the highway, a major earthquake began. The horses were disorientated, and Craig's horse fell down. Craig was able to jump out of the horse's way before it rolled onto its side. The earth was heaving up and down and sideways and it was all very unnerving for everyone. People came running out of their houses so quickly that suddenly Craig and Amel were just two of many on the street. When the quake stopped the horses were very upset, and so were Craig and Amel, so it was hard to get the horses to settle down. The scream of a woman in the distance warned of someone having been hurt. The people were slow to start moving back towards their houses to look at any possible damage. The few cars on the street started moving again.

Craig and Amel mounted their horses again and continued up the street towards the Chapel of the Holy Cross. As they started up the approach, there was another earthquake. Once again they had to dismount and they were terrified.

After the shaking had stopped and they were able to gather their wits about them and had calmed the horses, they noticed that a rock wall had appeared several yards in front of them, an abrupt obstacle to their progress. Craig was discouraged to the point of tears when suddenly he heard a calm voice.

'Oh Craig, you can do it. Just climb the wall and walk into the chapel with the stone.' It sounded like Marie.

"Amel, can you keep the horses while I climb this rock wall and walk up to the chapel?"

"Do you think that's wise?" Amel asked with trepidation in his voice.

"We have to complete what we came here to do," Craig answered.

"Okay, and God speed." Amel took the reins of Craig's horse.

Craig had the stone already in his pocket, and he quickly climbed what was only a five-foot rock wall. It had appeared more formidable when he first saw it. As he walked up the street toward the chapel there was another tremor. He stopped and spread his legs bracing for what he thought might be another big quake. The quake quickly stopped, but he had already had more fearful thoughts when he heard the voice again.

'We're all counting on you to get the ruby back into its proper place, and we know you can do it.'

It definitely was Marie's voice, and Craig decided to respond. 'I only need about ten more minutes. If only the earth would stop shaking,' he thought.

'Just keep taking steps towards the chapel and the altar.' Marie's voice again.

Craig now was able to quickly move towards the chapel and soon was inside. As he approached the altar, there was another quake, and it felt awful to be inside the building as it appeared to tumble about. This time, instead of stopping and bracing himself, he struggled to continue towards the altar. Under the altar on the backside, he found the panel that opened and the place where he could hang the ruby. The shaking continued, and he lay down alongside the altar, praying that the quaking would stop.

'Try to hang the ruby.' Marie's voice was in his head again.

'I'm waiting until the quaking stops,' Craig thought.

"The quaking will probably stop when you get the ruby into its place."

Craig tried now to get the stone out of his pocket, and when he moved it into the zone where it was going to be hung, the quaking stopped.

'Incredible,' he thought.

Craig finished hanging the ruby, stood up, and felt an overwhelming sense of accomplishment.

'I did it!' he thought to himself.

'Yea!' Marie's voice rang in his mind. 'I'm so glad and so proud of you!'

'I'm proud of me, too,' Craig thought.

As he walked out into the mountain air, he felt like he had a new spring in his step.

"I did it!" he shouted to Amel, who was struggling to keep the horses calm, and did not respond to Craig as he continued to talk to the horses.

Craig walked down to the place with the rock wall in the road, jumped off the rock wall and soon was standing next to Amel and the horses. The horses were calm and Amel answered, "I hope the ruby in its berth helps keep the earth calm. I can't take much more of this."

"Can your legs take some more saddle time?" Craig asked.

"They don't want to, but they are willing if we have to."

"Let's ride back through the Verde Valley," Craig said as he climbed his steed.

'God speed.' It was Marie's voice.

As soon as Amel mounted, they started back down the street and continued to ride south on Highway 179 towards the Verde Valley.

CHAPTER ELEVEN

The Way Back

Like migrating birds,
Horses and adventurers
Make their way back to a safer place.

Back at Pine there had been a rush of activity. Refugees from Phoenix were arriving hourly and there were numerous makeshift camps throughout the Payson area including Pine. Marie and her friends had decided to allow 12 people to stay at her site, and they were organizing those people to go out and help others. Getting enough water and toilet facilities was a major issue and temporary septic systems and outhouses were being built. Water had to be hauled from areas where either mountain streams or well-water could be accessed.

:::::

When the truck ran out of gas by Mormon Lake, Mencini only had to sit along the road a short while before an older fellow and his wife stopped and picked him up. They took him to the Flagstaff airport. He had a lot of cash on himself and was able to buy a ticket without using a credit card. He reasoned it would be harder for the authorities to track where he was if he could limit his identification trails. He also had false identification so he could travel under the psuedonym of Harvey Wallace. He had to wait about four hours before he was able to get on a flight to Alburquerque, where he hoped to get a plane to Houston, and then to the Cayman Islands. He wasn't worried about an Indian and a middle-aged man reporting their truck stolen, because the police had enough on their plate dealing with the earthquake.

When he was at the Alburquerque airport, he found out that the Cayman Islands were being inundated with a tsunami that was generated from the earthquakes. Mencini took a room at the

Ramada Inn close to the airport. There had not been much earthquake activity in Alburquerque so all the utilities were working and he enjoyed a long hot shower before laying down on the bed and falling fast asleep.

:::::::

This was the third day they had been riding the horses and their legs were very sore. Also, the horses needed food. By the time they got to the village of Oak Creek, they decided they should look for feed for the horses and take a break. After all, it would probably take a couple days to get back to Pine, so they had better keep up their strength.

They were able to ride their horses to the creek on the east side of the Outlets of Sedona and let them drink. Although the creek had stopped running because of the disruption to the terrain, there were still pools of water at the bottom of the creek.

There was a hardware store in the mall area along the highway. They stopped there and asked about oats for the horses and were given directions to a place about two blocks away. They also asked about a restaurant that might be open for business.

No one was surprised they were riding horses because there were other horse owners doing the same.

The man working at the store was very pleasant and accomodating. He explained, "After the recent earthquakes, most of the places around here don't have electricity or water. We've sold all of our standby generators and other hardware that people need to jerry-rig things so they can keep their homes and places going. There is one restaurant that is trying to make things work. They have an outdoor fireplace that they've made into a grill that they've been cooking on. It's the Sunset Lookout place on Verde Valley School Road."

Amel and Craig went to the feed store first and got oats for their horses and they also bought some alfalfa pellets. Then they rode over to the Sunset Lookout and found a place to tie up their horses and feed them before going into the restaurant. The place was very busy.

"I believe it will take us most of the remainder of the day to get to Camp Verde, where we can spend the night. I think it is over 15 miles from here, and I don't think I can ride much more than that today."

"Ride? After I eat, I want to take a nap," Amel smiled.

While sitting in the restaurant and listening to the conversation at the tables around them, they learned more about the extensive damage that the earthquakes had done. Telephones and electricity as well as water services were absent in much of the city. Where the water was working, people would carry jugs and pails to get water to bring back to their homes.

After their lunch, they rode the rest of the day to cover the 15 plus miles to Camp Verde, located along the I-17 highway by the Highway 260 access. The sky was overcast with gray clouds and the temperatures hovered in a temperate range and still they stopped every hour to rest for half an hour. After all the extra adrenalin their bodies experienced during the trauma of the earthquake, they were exhausted.

They encountered stragglers heading towards Sedona and the high country. Many of these people were traveling in trucks, and from conversations with some of these people, they learned that I-17 was badly damaged in areas, and only high clearance four-wheel drive vehichles were able to travel because they had to drive over large cracks and debris and go off road in places. There were many people below the worst damaged areas, and there was a makeshift refugee camp set-up on the north side of Phoenix.

When they stopped to rest, Amel and Craig talked about what had happened and how they could communicate with their thoughts only.

In the town of Camp Verde they were able to learn that there was a rancher on the east side of town who would agree to let them camp out on the edge of his property and sell them some fodder for their horses. Amel and Craig were very sensitive to any gut feelings their bodies might tell them about the accomodations, but everything seemed all right. Soon after staking out their horses and pitching their tent, they were fast asleep.

When they woke up it was past sun-up and they were stiff and sore. They decided to get their horses saddled up and ride over to a restaurant in Camp Verde for breakfast before heading east towards Pine.

While they were in the restaurant, they were surprised to see Standing Bear pull up, park his rusty red truck with a horse trailer behind it, and come inside.

"Standing Bear! You're a wonderful sight this fine morning!" Craig said while he and Amel both enthusiastically greeted Standing Bear.

"Hrmm. I thought you fellows might be tired of riding horseback, so I decided to come and get you." Standing Bear stood beaming.

"But how did you know where to find us?" Amel asked.

"I let my spirit guide lead me to you," Standing Bear said with a sparkle in his eyes.

"Sit down and have a cup of coffee with us before we do anything else," Craig said.

Standing Bear sat down with the duo and listened to their story.

"It's been close to 24 hours since you hung that ruby, and the earth has been still since then. I'd say that is more than a coincidence." Amel looked at Craig and smiled.

"I hope it stays quiet for a while. We've got a lot to do to help people, who have been displaced from the tragic destruction in Phoenix."

After having a pleasant visit and coffee, the trio went outside and opened the back of the horse trailer and led the two horses into it. Then they got into the truck and headed east on Highway 260 towards Pine.

During the ride Amel and Craig learned more about what was going on at Marie's.

CHAPTER TWELVE

At Marie's Camp

In the morning sun
A flock of Pelicans gather.
About one hundred.

Along the ride to Marie's Camp Standing Bear told them about the efforts to create a sustainable living community in Pine and Strawberry. There were a lot of refugees from Phoenix, and plans were well underway to keep them for a long duration, as it could take a long time to rebuild some parts of the city.

They had started to develop systems for caring for the expanded community. Finding enough water was one problem, and simple tasks such as gathering and distributing food had become challenging. A bigger problem was health care as some people had sustained injuries and others had chronic illnesses such as diabetes.

The local gas stations had hooked up standby generators to run their pumps, but the future supply of gasoline was uncertain as so many refineries and transportation systems had been damaged.

They were fortunate in that they had been able to get a car and a truck that was powered by a Haye's hydrogen engine, and they only needed batteries to run the engines, which had alternators that recharged the batteries as they went along. The mechanical engineer, Jim Thoreau, was able to keep the hydrogen-powered car and truck repaired and operating. Marie had solar collectors that could charge up any dead batteries if need be. These tools would become even more necessary if the gas supplies were to run dry, and that could happen within a few weeks because all the refineries in Texas were shut down. There were a lot fewer cars and trucks driving around and that was stretching out the existing local fuel supply.

They brought the horses back to Charley's place.

By the time they got to Marie's it was time for lunch. They joined a group of about 25 people under a large tent that had been erected in Marie's front yard.

Marie was in the house helping with the food preparation, and when she came outside and saw them, she quickly came over to greet them.

"How are my favorite cowboys and Indian doing?" she beamed.

"Glad to be out of the saddle," Amel offered.

"And we're really glad to be safely back here," Craig said.

"Well, come over here and sit down and tell me about your adventure," Marie said as she led them to a place at a makeshift table with benches.

Food was brought to them, and Craig and Amel took turns telling about what had happened as they ate. While she listened, Marie would nod approval at parts of the story where decisions had been made or offer astonished looks and pitiful sounds where encounters with difficult people had occurred. Craig let her know how helpful it was to hear her voice when he struggled to get the ruby to the chapel place.

"I was praying for you and Amel frequently when you were on the mission," she said. "And I could hear your voice in my head when you were struggling, so I sent you thoughts of encouragement. I'm so glad that I was able to be useful to you."

When the story was over, Craig asked about the telephone system. He had not heard anything about what was happening back in Minnesota and he was anxious to communicate with his family and friends there.

"Is there any chance that the telephone system is working again? I would like to call Minnesota," Craig said.

"Yes, some people were using their phones this morning."

"Well, my cell phone is dead. Is there anyone who has a phone that I could use?"

Marie said she would find one, and went off looking for a phone, while Craig and Amel finished their meal. A cup of hot tea was also brought to them and they were thoroughly enjoying being at a place that felt like home.

When Craig got a telephone, he called his son Dan directly.

"Boy am I glad to hear your voice," Craig said.

"I feel the same way," his son Dan said. "We've been wondering what had happened to you. It's been five days since the big earthquake hit the Western United States, and there's been a lot of people injured. How are you anyway?"

"Physically, I'm okay. I've been helping people at a camp north of Phoenix at a place called Pine," Craig explained.

"How's everybody doing?"

"Everybody's fine here," Dan explained. "But a lot of families down there are not. We heard from Joe that Aunt Florence and her son Mike are presumed to be dead, and Joe and Larry have been hurt badly. Some of the other cousins are trying to get back to Minnesota. The problem is the Phoenix airport is completely out of commission, so they have to make their way to Albuquerque or Las Vegas if they want to catch a flight this way. The second part of the problem is that the planes are filled up and you have to wait for days to get a seat."

"At some point, I'll have to think about making my way back."

"Well, we'd like to see you sooner than later," Dan said.

"I'm going to see what I can do to get back, and will let you know what I find out."

After he hung up, Craig called his boss and found out that his boss was anxious to have him back too.

When Marie learned that Craig was planning to return to Minnesota, she had a talk with him. "So far Minnesota has not had a catastrophic happening. Would you like to do something to help ensure that will continue?"

"Sure, as long as it doesn't involve danger, or horseback riding," Craig smiled.

"I had a vision of Minnesota with all its wonderful waters," Marie continued. "And in the vision a crow brought a beautiful crystal to a water spring and buried it in the ground towards the sunrise direction. As soon as the crystal was in the ground, a beautiful multi-colored sunrise occurred."

"Wow! That does sound powerful. What do you think it means?"

"My guess is that you represent the crow."

"Me! Why?"

"Because the crow is a family of birds that you have identified with in an earlier period, and you are the only one who fits that description that I know is planning on going to Minnesota."

"Okay. Let's say that the crow does represent me. What else could the dream mean?"

"It could mean that you know of a spring in Minnesota that some people consider sacred, and you could bring a crystal there and bury it in the ground on the sunrise side. What risk is there in that?"

"Where would I find such a powerful crystal?"

"I just happen to have one here," Marie giggled as she pulled a small blue velvet cloth bag out of her pocket. She opened it so Craig could see the blue crystal inside the bag.

When she handed the blue crystal and the small blue velvet cloth bag to Craig she said, "Here you go, if you choose to accept this mission."

"Okay. It seems easy enough. Can't hurt anything."

"God bless you," Marie said in a sincere way. Then she gave him a big hug.

After talking with members of the group at Marie's, Craig learned that he could get a ride to Holbrook in the hydrogen-powered car, and from there he could catch another ride to Albuquerque through a local small plane service that operated out of Holbrook.

As Craig was preparing to leave, Standing Bear took him aside. "Hrmm. I want to talk with you alone for a few minutes."

They walked over to a quiet place on the outskirts of the camp.

"Hrmm. I had a vision of you getting in trouble again," Standing Bear began. "I want to give you something to help you. I know you don't like the gun, and you can't take one on a plane anyway, so I've prepared some strong medicine for you." And he handed Craig a small cloth bag, but before Craig could take it, he held it in the palm of his hand and opened it up so Craig could see what was inside. There were three small vials.

"This one has a screw cap, and you take it off like this," said Standing Bear as he unscrewed the vial. "There is a needle on the end that you can poke into someone's skin; if you then squeeze the side of the plastic vial, they get real sick in a few minutes. It's part rattlesnake venom. And this one with the little cork on the end holds some powder, which if ingested will cause a person to become paralyzed for about 30 minutes. I am giving you an extra one of these, in case you need more time. I suggest carrying this bag in your pocket, because you never know when you might need this to deal with a bad man."

Craig took the small bag of potent drugs and thanked Standing bear. "Hopefully, we will get to see each other again in less troubled times," he said and then gave him a big hug. Afterwards, he wondered what kind of trouble Standing Bear had foreseen for him.

There were two other people in the group that also wanted to go to Holbrook, and it was decided to send Amel with the hydrogen-powered car.

CHAPTER THIRTEEN
Across Country

Over the water
Low and easterly
A blue Heron soars

Getting to Albuquerque would prove to be interesting. Once there, however, there would be options to travel further east. Besides the Albuquerque International Sunport that was still functioning, the Amtrack train was running from Albuquerque to Chicago and from Chicago across Minnesota all the way to Montana. The routes through the Rocky Mountains were badly damaged from all the earthquakes, but east of the Rockies there was minimal damage.

They left late morning the following day because they learned they would not be able to catch a flight to Albuquerque until late afternoon; and it would only take them about an hour and a half to get to Holbrook.

They took Highway 87 to Payson and then Highway 260 east of Payson until they got to Highway 377 just east of Heber, where they turned north towards Holbrook. Along the way they encountered a few cars, but saw more pickup trucks with their back cargo boxes piled up with various items.

After about two and a half hours they were at the Holbrook airport. Only one of the fellows, who wanted to go to Holbrook, was accompanying Craig on his flight to Albuquerque. The other was going to run an errand with Amel and return back to Pine.

While buying their tickets and waiting to board the airplane, Craig was surprise and delighted to see a blonde-haired woman that he recognized. It was Sally, whose car he had helped jump-start about six days ago on highway 87.

"Fancy meeting you here," Craig said when he walked up to her.

At first she squinted her eyes and cocked her head to one side while she studied him. "Do I know you?"

"Yes, I helped you start your car on Highway 87 by the earthquake fault about six days ago."

Then her eyes lit up and she smiled. "Oh sure! I recognize you now. Where is your Indian friend?"

"Oh, he's back in Pine. I'm trying to get back to Minnesota, and he is staying to help with the disaster relief."

"What a coincidence. I'm going to Minnesota, too," she exclaimed.

They started visiting, and Sally learned of Craig's adventures, and Craig learned more about Sally. After she had left Craig and Standing Bear on Highway 87, Sally had returned to Phoenix and tried to get to her friend's house to help her with the aftermath of the earthquake, but wasn't able to get there. She ended up helping with a relief effort at the refugee camp that was set up along east Shea Boulevard in Phoenix. After a couple days, she realized that she wanted to return to Minnesota so she could be with her family there.

It took her two days to make her way to Holbrook.

Craig was feeling a strong connection to this woman and felt attracted to her. Sally was having similar feelings, and after a brief time of conversation they realized that they could read each other's mind.

It started when Craig thought, 'Boy, she's hot!'

And Sally said, 'What do you mean by hot?'

Craig was used to this phenomenon and he just answered by thinking, 'like a warm summer day.'

Sally smiled and thought, 'Relaxing at the beach.'

Craig looked at her, smiled, and said, 'Yeaaaah.'

Soon they boarded the plane, and in the late afternoon flight they traveled to Albuquerque together. They both were carrying backpacks only. The flight was brief, lasting about 45 minutes.

The sun was shining in Albuquerque when they landed, and when they entered the airport terminal it felt like they had returned to civilization after their long ordeal in Arizona.

Unfortunately, the wait for a plane to Minnesota, or anywhere for that matter, was going to be several days, so they started to look at their other options. There was a public notice bulletin board that had been erected in the main lobby of the airport. There were many notices of owners of RVs, trucks, and other vehicles offering to take passengers to many places in the United States. There was a group of volunteers working to coordinate these voyages.

When Craig and Sally asked about one modified charter bus, they learned it had enough extra fuel to go all the way to Chicago. They followed this lead, and after talking with the driver on the phone, they agreed to meet him at a truck stop on the east side of Albuquerque the next morning.

Sally and Craig were also able to find a motel room not far from the truck stop and they shared the same room, but not the same bed. They were just traveling together and getting to know one another and they were both comfortable with that.

Sally learned about Craig's life in Minnesota and she shared some about her life there.

"I was a nurse for about eighteen years at the Methodist Hospital in St. Louis Park," she began. "I had a hard-working husband, and thought that we would grow old together and retire in the south. He was unfaithful, however, and I sought a divorce. I stayed around for a couple years after the divorce, and tried to make a new life for myself there. Eventually, I decided I needed a whole new start and so I moved to Phoenix and got work there. That's where I've been for about four years, working at the St. Joseph Children's hospital. About two weeks ago I decided to quit that job and take a new job in California. When the earthquake hit California so hard, I knew I couldn't get there. I felt compelled to go north and get out of the city and enjoy the high country for a while when the Phoenix earthquake hit. I guess I should feel like a refugee, but I don't. I feel liberated and ready for a fresh start and a new adventure."

Craig liked the optimistic attitude that Sally had, and he thought as much. She looked demurely at him and smiled.

The next morning, they arose in time to go and meet their unusual transportation, which was at a truck stop close to where Central Avenue (old Route 66) connected with Interstate 40 on the east side of Albuquerque. They had to walk about a mile. The fellow who had the modified charter bus was a tall man with a potbelly. He wore a cowboy-cut red shirt, and jeans and the jeans were kept up with a belt around his low waist below his potbelly. He wore a blue baseball hat that had a logo on it that said, "Buy American." There were ten other people there. The charter bus was a half-bus with a fifth wheel on the back and was pulling a medium-sized trailer. The cabin of the bus had a bathroom and bed and table with cushioned benches.

"Now I'm not offering you all the most comfortable of rides, but since I want to get back to the Midwest, and I don't have a back-haul, it occurred to me that I could help out you all and still get paid. So, like the ad said, I want $200 apiece from each of you and I'll take you to most any point between here and Chicago. There should be plenty of fresh air, and I'll stop every two hours so people can stretch their legs." He said all this with an easy going manner, and he seemed like a real affable fellow. He reminded Craig of Slim Pickens.

Both Craig and Sally felt good about him and decided to commit; they gave him $200 apiece. All of the other people there did the same thing. The inside of the cabin looked comfortable enough. There was barely room for twelve people. Under the table was a large cooler of bottled water with paper cups, and a box full of sundry items like tissues, toilet paper and peanuts.

"Just like the airlines," Tall Man said with a big smile.

The bus with its trailer was soon heading east on Interstate 40. Within an hour they were close to Clines Corners.

:::::::

Mencini had waited in Albuquerque for over four days and grew impatient waiting for a flight to Atlanta, where he hoped to catch a plane to Bogotá, Columbia. Frustrated, he decided to seek other alternative transportation and discovered there was a private charter air company with a flight scheduled to Atlanta, and they had room for one more. He decided to go that route even though it would cost him $2,500. He felt anxious to get out of the United States and was carrying enough cash to survive in a South American economy for some time. Eventually, he hoped that the assets he had in the Cayman Island bank could be recovered, since the bank invested most of their assets in areas around the world.

The plane was scheduled to leave in the morning, and he was delighted to be boarding the small plane. His carry-on bag contained most of his cash, and he also had checked a bag that had some more of it. When he got to his seat, he stuffed his carry-on under the seat in front of him so he could keep an eye on it. There were eleven other passengers, a flight attendant, and a pilot and co-pilot. After a pre-flight check up, the plane taxied away from the concourse to wait in line to take off.

When the airplane took off everything seemed perfect. The plane rose into the air like a normal takeoff. Mencini felt very relieved to finally be on his way again, and the mood of the other passengers seemed to be the same as the plane lifted up into the air leaving Albuquerque and New Mexico behind. However, shortly after the plane was in the air, the pilot announced that there was some problem with the plane and they would have to return and get the problem fixed. When the plane was banking a turn low to the ground to avoid the busy skies overhead, one of the airfoil controls jammed and the pilot lost control of the plane as it began to slide out of its banking pattern and closer to the ground. The pilot was able to pull off enough correction to bring the plane belly down onto Interstate 40 just east of Clines Corners.

::::::

When Tall Man saw the plane headed towards him he grunted, "Oh shit," and turned the direction of his truck to the opposite side of the highway towards which the plane seemed to be heading. The plane started turning on its belly and careened out of control into the left ditch as Tall Man brought his truck to a stop in the right ditch about 100 yards from the plane. There had been a lot of sparks created from the fuselage of the plane skidding along the concrete highway, and a small fire had started on the left wing.

Tall Man put out a 911 call on his cell phone. Some of the passengers got out of the bus. They were flabbergasted to see the wrecked plane with a small fire burning.

"I don't see anyone getting out. Maybe we should go and get some of the passengers out of there."

"Are you crazy? That plane is likely to blow up at anytime."

One of the passengers headed towards the wreck, and Craig decided to join him.

"We're going to go see if we can help," Craig said as he took off, and the two of them started running.

Soon three more of the bus passengers followed after them, while Tall Man and the less brave souls stayed with the bus.

::::::

The mood in the airplane had quickly turned to disappointment and then to fear as the plane started to turn around and then, within minutes, crash along Interstate 40. The sound of the fuselage rubbing on the concrete was loud and awful, like chalk being rubbed the wrong way on a blackboard.

After the plane had stopped, there was some confusion as to how to get out of the plane. Quickly it was decided that the exit door opposite the burning wing was the best escape, even if that side of the plane was elevated more off the ground. As a couple of passengers tried to open the door, the flight attendant came and helped with that task. Meanwhile, the pilot and copilot had not yet come out of their cabin and the flight attendant decided to check on their situation. None of the passengers were hurt badly and they had started to exit the plane when the rescuers from the truck came running up. Mencini was not one of the first passengers out of the plane.

::::::

About half of the passengers were out of the plane and far enough away to avoid injury when the large explosion happened. The entire fuel tank ignited in the damaged wing, and the explosion sent everybody nearby flying off their feet and onto the ground. The noise from the explosion caused temporary damage to his ears, so Craig could not understand what others were saying, but he decided to get up and bring one other person with him.

He went to the person closest to him and helped him to his feet, and then they limped away from the burning plane towards the truck. When they got near the bus there were others from the bus that came forward to help them and others coming from the plane. Craig realized he was also hurt and bleeding from the left side of his head. People were milling about in a chaotic manner. Some of the injured decided to lie down. A couple were carried towards the truck and then laid down.

Sally finally stepped away from the group, turned and talked to the group in a louder voice. "Ahem," she cleared her throat. "Hopefully, an emergency response unit will be here soon. Meanwhile, it is important that we get everyone in a safe position. I'm a nurse, so I know what to do. Is there anyone else here who has emergency response training?"

The rest of the group said nothing to answer the question. Meanwhile, Sally had started to check the people that were lying down.

Craig felt nauseous and sat down by the bus. Mencini was also among the injured, only he was lying down and Craig could not see him.

A rescue squad arrived from the nearby community of Clines Corners, but they did not have an ambulance and could only administer first aid and help prepare people for transport. When the first ambulance arrived, the people injured worst were taken. Mencini was in that group.

Craig was in the second group and he didn't have much time to talk to Sally. "I'll call you when we get back to Minnesota."

Sally was anxious and she looked down for a moment before answering. "Okay. Give me one of your business cards so I can call you too."

The ride to the Albuquerque Hospital was a blur in Craig's mind. He was feeling ill, and the medics were fussing with him and talking and it all seem to happen fast. After he was in the hospital he went through a long period in the waiting area where he was monitored for a variety of conditions before being taken to an MRI unit for a brain scan.

During this time, Craig was in and out of a fearful state and was unable to contact any of his friends through telepathy. He remembered to pray and that brought him to a place of peace momentarily. However, being around the other people who were in various states of suffering caused him to be empathetic towards their suffering and that also restricted his ability to connect telepathically with others.

Eventually he was admitted to the hospital where he stayed for two nights.

Mencini was also admitted as Harvey Wallace, the pseudonym under which he was traveling. When the hospital personnel did an inventory of his belongings and discovered that he was carrying large amounts of cash, they informed the police. He was investigated, and because it was an airplane crash, there were federal investigators involved. They were able to link him to the infamous Al Mencini and he was arrested while still in his hospital bed. When he was released from the hospital a few days later, he was accompanied by the federal investigators. However, he never made it to the county jail. Instead, the federal investigators turned him over to the CIA.

When Craig checked out of the hospital two days after the plane crash, he was feeling very rested and fit to travel. The social worker at the hospital had arranged for him to get on a faster moving queue for an airplane flight to Minnesota, and he was able to catch a flight within 36 hours of his release. He spent one night at a hotel near the hospital before going to the airport.

CHAPTER FOURTEEN

A Spring in Minnesota

By the babbling brook
The boughs of pussy willows
Sway in the soft breeze

By the time Craig returned to Minnesota, he learned Sally had also arrived. She had gone as far as St. Louis with Tall Man and the bus and trailer rig. From St. Louis she had caught a plane to Minneapolis, where she arrived just a day before Craig.

Sally was staying with friends in Hopkins and they met at the C-10 restaurant on Main Street shortly after Craig arrived in Minnesota. When he had left Minnesota a couple of weeks ago, Craig had parked his car in the parking lot of a local business, who was a client, in the Minnetonka industrial park off of Highway 169, just south of Hopkins. It was easy for him to stop in Hopkins after he arrived. He was delighted to discover Sally was so close.

While enjoying food and beer at the restaurant, they chatted for some time. During that conversation, Craig told Sally of the request he had from Marie to bury the blue crystal he had with him on the sunrise side of a sacred spring. The one spring he thought might fit that description was the Coldwater Spring in a wooded area off of Hiawatha Avenue, south of Minnehaha Park between the Mississippi River and Hiawatha Avenue on the north side of the Ft. Snelling property. This was the last natural spring in all of Hennepin County, a large metropolitan county. The spring's location was close to the meeting place of the Minnesota and Mississippi Rivers and its waters flowed into the only gorge on the Mississippi River. There had been summer solstice and winter solstice celebrations there by a local Wicca group and other earth friendly spiritualists in the past. Craig had attended one of these ceremonies and was familiar with the location.

Coldwater has been flowing at least 10,000 years. Native Americans have legally recognized sacred site rights at majestic landscapes like Coldwater. The local Native American groups had argued for years for this area to become a park area and to be protected as such. There was only one other sacred spring in Hennepin County, the Great Medicine Spring in Theodore Wirth Park, and it was permanently dewatered with construction of Interstate 394 in the late 1980s.

Meanwhile, the weather had not been clear for some time.

The volcanic eruptions along the Pacific Rim, both in California and in Asia, caused many tons of particulates to enter the atmosphere. The result was many days of totally cloud-filled skies. Many of the communication satellites became ineffective because all the sulfur and other particulates in the atmosphere were altering the digital information.

The contamination of the atmosphere by all the particulates was also hindering the use of engines of all types. Although traditional internal combustion engines could work, the ashes and other particulates would quickly plug the air filters, and running those engines without filters would cause them to wear out quickly. People had to frequently replace air filters or frequently have them cleaned. It became common to check air filters with every gas tank filling.

Air traffic was becoming very expensive because the engines were having more wear as a result of the jet engines sucking in so many particulates. The price of the passenger seats tripled. Fewer people willing to pay the exorbitant prices and there were fewer flights. The result was limited communication and fewer transportation choices.

Craig was glad he was back in Minnesota as the economy worsened because of the changes to the earth. He was also glad he had met Sally and he hoped his time would be less lonely in Minnesota. He planned to go to Flat Prairie for a few days. When he returned to Minneapolis she agreed to join him for a visit to the spring by Hiawatha Avenue and afterwards they would go out for dinner.

Back in Flat Prairie there were a lot of changes. Craig's company, Safe n' Sound, was in crisis, because so many of their systems had been damaged. The digital banking systems were in chaos due to systems damaged because of the earthquakes in the south, southwest and west coast. This was causing problems with both payables and receivables. Safe n' Sound had not been able to assess where all the damage had been and it appeared as though that process could take months. Craig's boss was glad he was back so he could help assess the kinds of system damage they could expect and help coordinate a recovery process.

Many people in Flat Prairie had relatives who had suffered loss or physical injury or death because of the catastrophes. There were several funeral or memorial services planned and some of them were for multiple deceased. Some people were so upset by the changes in the climate and the catastrophes that they had started hoarding supplies and boarding themselves in their homes. Other people responded by being sympathetic with the distressed and offering condolences, help and support. Most people were affected in some way.

Gas rationing had started. People had to wait in line and they could only buy 10 gallons of gas at a time.

After three days, Craig finally returned to Minneapolis. He was anxious to see Sally again and he had been unable to communicate with her telepathically. After contacting her by phone and making arrangements to meet her, they had been able to resume telepathic communication. They weren't sure of the reason for the lapse in telepathic communication, but assumed it was because they were putting a lot of their attention on other aspects of their lives and not on one another.

They decided to meet at the C-10 restaurant again and Sally would then accompany Craig to the spring off of Hiawatha Avenue.

It was a pleasant fall day. The leaves on the trees had all turned color and there was a variety of golden brown, golden, yellow, green and red-leaved trees. The air was calm and it felt like a grand day to be on an adventure.

When they arrived at the Coldwater Spring's location, Craig decided to park the car about a block away from the gate and out of sight of the complex. Sally agreed to wait in the car and to let Craig know if anyone with authority arrived while he was inside. When Craig discovered that the gate to the area was locked, he decided to ignore the "No Trespassing" sign, climbed over the gate, and walked over to the spring area.

It was a short walk, and he arrived there shortly after he was out of Sally's sight. There was an area just northeast of the spring that at one time had a labyrinth. Craig decided what looked like the center of where the labyrinth used to be would be an ideal spot to bury the blue crystal, since the sunrise would be occurring in that general direction during the summer solstice. He thought to Sally, 'I'm here and have found a place to bury the crystal,' hoping she would be able to pick up on his thoughts.

'God bless you,' Sally thought back.

A crow flew into the labyrinth circle and landed between Craig and the spring.

Using the small garden spade he had brought from the car, Craig buried the crystal in a manner that left little evidence by opening a slit in the soil, slipping the crystal into the earth, and then stepping down on it.

The crow lifted up into the air and let out a loud "Caw!" as Craig was stepping away from the site. Then a loud voice yelled out, "Hey, what are you doing there?"

Craig stopped and turned towards the direction from which he thought he had heard the voice and yelled, "Having a contemplative moment." He managed to slip the small spade in his back pocket in a discreet manner.

There was a pregnant pause, and Craig thought to Sally, 'We've got company.'

From the direction of the large building to the northeast of the spring, a fellow with a medium build in a tan, zipped-up jacket and a black baseball cap came walking briskly towards him.

When he got close, Craig could see he was stern-faced and brandishing a holstered pistol, which was on a belt around his hip. A badge on his jacket identified him as a security police person.

"This is a secure area and you are trespassing," the man said.

"This is a public spring and I have a right to be here." Craig was trying to remain calm, but felt some fear. He fidgeted with the bottom of his jacket so that the back side of his jacket covered the exposed part of the garden spade in his back pocket.

"I have called my boss and they are sending someone to come and get you, and you will be charged with trespassing."

Craig thought of Sally and was anxious, but didn't want her to feel that, so he tried to maintain a calm thought.

Then Craig said to the guard, "Well, I understand you have to do what you are ordered to do, but I haven't done anything wrong here. Couldn't you just let me go?"

"No. There are people coming now, and they already know you are here."

'People?' Craig thought to himself so loud that he was afraid the guard may have heard him think. 'Why is this guard not saying, 'police'?'

And then two men in dark suits came from the direction of the building. They came up to Craig and ordered him to come with them. With one man on each side of him and the security guard behind, they walked briskly towards the building and entered through a door on its south side.

This building was called Building 9, and was abandoned by the U.S. Bureau of Mines in 1995. It was a library building for the rest of the 11-building campus, which had been unused and deteriorating since 1995. Some of the old campus had been torn down, and one building was currently undergoing demolition.

Craig thought it was odd that these people were using the building, because he had believed that the building had been vacant for some time, and it was in bad disrepair. Since this building was on government property he assumed there was probably a covert government operation being staged there.

Inside the building, the hallways were not lighted and it was hard to see ahead of them. The building had a strong, dank, musty smell. As they walked down the hallway, there was one man ahead of him and one alongside; the security guard had stayed outside.

Craig was thinking about a possible escape as he did not like the way this was feeling. The men were very gruff and non-conversational. There was an exaggerated sense of authority about them; and it did not feel honest.

Soon they were entering a lighted room. Inside was a table with chairs around it. On one side of the room was a mirrored window. 'An interrogation room,' Craig thought.

"Sit down," one of the black-suited men said gruffly.

Craig sat down so he could see the door to his left. He was trying to remain very calm, and was praying for courage and strength. He was getting a strong notion from his inner self that he should escape. The garden spade was still sticking out of his pocket and he was surprised that these men had not frisked him, yet. One of the men stood by the door while the other sat down across from him. Craig now had a moment to study him more. He was a middle-aged man with a brown head of hair and a goatee and black-rimmed glasses. His nose was narrow and he leaned towards Craig when he spoke.

"Let's make this as expedient as possible," he said. "I want to know why you are here today. You will tell us, and then we will charge you with trespassing and let you go. Okay?"

Craig nodded his head.

"Why are you here today?"

"To balance the ley lines that flow through this location," Craig answered. He didn't want to have the blue crystal disappear, and he buried it in such a way as to make it hard to be discovered. He didn't think anyone would find it unless by accident, so he decided not to tell them about it.

"What kind of bullshit answer is that?" the interrogator asked in a raised voice.

"It's the same kind of respect for the natural earth forces that those who have come here for ceremonies would have," Craig answered.

"You guys are a pain in the ass," the man answered with a similarly loud voice seething with contempt. "Okay, show me your identification."

Craig did not have his wallet with him, and knew they weren't going to like his answer. "I don't have my ID with me. My name is Gus Moore. I'm from Minneapolis."

"Okay, we'll give you a ride to your home, and write you up for trespassing after you get your ID."

Craig felt relieved. He hadn't given the idea of lying about his identity any thought. It was just a reaction he had, because of an old habit of lying about his identity when he got into trouble when he was a young man. He hadn't been in a situation like this since he was a young man. It was almost as though he surprised himself.

He also liked the idea of being taken away from this ominous building, because then he would have a better chance to escape. They led him to another room that was a sparsely furnished office area. There was a desk and chairs, some file cabinets, a small kitchenette nook with coffee brewing, and a table and more chairs. The man, who had been doing all the talking, was named Pat. He poured himself a cup of coffee and asked Craig if he wanted one.

"There will be a little wait while we get the car. You can have a cup of coffee if you wish." He was more pleasant now. Craig decided to accept the offer.

From this office area, there was a window that looked out towards Minnehaha Park. Craig couldn't see his car, and he knew Sally would be anxious, so he thought to her, 'I'll be leaving this building site in a car soon. Please be ready to go.'

By now Craig had stood up and walked over to the window. One of the black-suited men said, "Please stay seated at that table." And he pointed to the table with the chairs.

Craig walked over to the table and sat down. A cup of coffee was handed to him. He fiddled with it, but it was still too hot. It occurred to Craig that they may be slipping him a drug, so he decided not to drink it. The fellow drinking coffee set his cup down on the table across from Craig and then walked over to the desk and picked up a telephone. He dialed a number, listened to the telephone for a moment, and hung up. He then looked out the window.

Craig could sense the fellow's thoughts weren't good. The fellow was thinking, 'We should just waste this guy. He already has seen more than we want him to. I think somewhere off the property would be best.'

Craig was very concerned that his life was in danger.

The other fellow stood by the door watching Craig and then walked over to the window and looked out. While these men were moving about, Craig had a chance to slip some of the powder Standing Bear had given him into his antagonist's cup of coffee. Eventually the fellow came back to his cup of coffee, picked it up and drank it.

A moment later, the other fellow, Bert, happened to be looking out of the window and he announced, "The car is ready and Sam is opening the gate."

"Good," the coffee drinking fellow said. "Bring Gus here out to the car and take him home. And then write him up after he gives you his identification."

Bert, who appeared to be second in command, walked up to Craig and said, "Okay, let's go."

Craig got up and followed him out of the room and down the hallway and towards the door to the outside. Shortly after they left the coffee drinking fellow alone, he went into a paralyzed state.

Craig got into the car with Bert. The other fellow in a black suit, Sam, was in the driver's seat. Craig was directed to sit on the passenger side, and Bert, who led him out of the building, sat in the back seat behind him. While Craig got into the car, he was able to slip his garden spade under the passenger seat. Then they drove through the gate, stopped, and Sam, the driver, got out and walked back to shut the gate. Craig noticed that the driver had an open can of soda pop in the console next to the shifting lever. When Bert in the back seat turned his head to watch his companion close the gate, Craig slipped some more white powder into the can of soda pop.

After Sam got back into the car, Bert said, "Okay, where do you live?"

Craig answered, "4908 Nokomis Avenue."

Sam drove the car out onto the street and crossed over Hiawatha Avenue and onto 53rd Street. Within a minute or so, Sam came to a stop at an intersection and then took a drink from his can of soda pop.

Meanwhile Craig could sense Bert in the back seat thinking bad thoughts. Bert was thinking, 'I think we'll just take this fellow over to the Phillips neighborhood and waste him in some alley, so that it looks like a drug deal gone bad. This should be easy. He seems like such a mellow dude.'

They drove through down 54th street, which went through a residential neighborhood that was established in the 1920s and 30s. By the time the group came to Nokomis Avenue, Sam went into a paralyzed state, but not before turning onto Nokomis Avenue and turning the wheel to the right to avoid a head-on collision with oncoming traffic.

Craig grabbed the wheel of the car and exclaimed, "Whoa, we got a problem here! Is your friend having a heart attack?"

"I don't know!" Bert answered loudly. "Try to brake the car and I'll get out and take over the driving."

Craig slipped his foot over the console and stepped on the brake pedal.

When Bert got out, Craig decided to make his move to escape. He stepped on the accelerator pedal and the car lurched ahead. Craig then steered the car down the street with his left hand as it quickly accelerated. He then had to slow down and make a left on 52nd Street where Nokomis runs into Keewaydin Park. After making that turn he stepped on the accelerator again for another block, and then slowed down again to turn right at the next street. He went speeding down that street until he got to 50th, where he turned left.

After turning onto 50th Street, he felt confident that he had lost his antagonist.

Then he arrived at a neighborhood retail area at 28th and 50th, parked the car a block away, got out, and walked back to the retail area. He entered a coffee shop called Coffee Café and ordered a cup of decaf coffee as calmly as he could. He was very shaken up and his body was filled with adrenalin. He wanted to get into a calmer state of mind so he could communicate with Sally, but the previous moment of escape kept repeatedly playing out in his mind. He decided to call her on his cell phone.

Craig was extremely grateful that Sally answered. "Where are you?" she asked.

"I'm at the Coffee Café on 50th and 28th Street."

"I'll be there in a moment."

Meanwhile, Bert, who had been running after Craig down Nokomis Avenue, had stopped and called back to headquarters. When his boss didn't answer, he became aware that they had been hoodwinked.

As he stood alongside Cedar Avenue, he yelled out loud, "Damn!"

::::::

When Sally arrived at the Coffee Café, they were both relieved.

"I just escaped from the men from that building and my system is pumped with adrenalin. I'm not comfortable being in this neighborhood now, so let's go somewhere else," Craig said without a pause in between the sentences.

Sally could tell he was still anxious and was relieved that he was okay. She was nervous and coughed before saying, "Let's get in your car and go then."

They got in Craig's car and drove west on 50th Avenue. When they got to Lake Nokomis they turned to the right and followed the road around the lake until they could cross over to Minnehaha Parkway. Craig kept driving west until he crossed the 35W interstate and they were in Tangle Town. They went down Lyndale Avenue to Lake Street where they turned left and headed to the Bryant Lake Bowl for a break. They drank beer for a while, and then decided to bowl a couple frames. Craig needed to do something to shake off the adrenaline.

"What do you think would have happened if you would have been honest with those men and not tried to escape?"

"For one thing I would have had to include you in the problem, because I had left my wallet in the car with you. Had I been honest with them I would have had to go to my car to get my wallet, and then you would have been implicated as an accomplice."

"So?"

"I just didn't feel good about those men." Craig shrugged his shoulders. "They were being too secretive. What are they doing there anyway? Besides, my hunches were right: I could hear them thinking and they were definitely planning my demise. The option to escape was obvious, because I had the special powders."

"That is interesting that Standing Bear gave you those powders," Sally said. She coughed before adding, "Are you sure that you were supposed to use them when you did?"

"No, I can't be sure; but I think it's a coincidence that when I am carrying out the mission that Marie asked me to do, that I would be accosted by these strange men on a mysterious mission of their own."

"I hope that is the end of that."

"Me too."

For the evening, Sally suggested that they go to a quiet restaurant and have a leisurely dinner. They settled on a place in St. Louis Park called Thanh Do, which is located off of Minnetonka

Boulevard. There they enjoyed the simple but elegant setting and tasted the Asian salad and spring rolls while sipping Pinot Grigio.

They spent the rest of the evening telling adventure stories from their youth. The longer they spent time together the more they enjoyed each other.

"If I wasn't staying with friends, you could stay with me tonight," Sally offered.

"I'd like that very much. Maybe we will have opportunities in the near future. You could always come out to Flat Prairie and visit me."

"I'll do that someday, but right now I have to find a job and get more settled in."

Because it had become so difficult to travel, Craig decided to take a room at a hotel by the Ridgedale shopping center.

The next day was Sunday and Craig slept in. When he got up, he walked around the shopping plaza for a while. He found a newspaper and a cup of coffee, then sat down and enjoyed the cup of coffee and read some of the newspaper before returning to Flat Prairie.

CHAPTER FIFTEEN
Evil in Minnesota

Shimmering water
Under a puffy white cloud sky
Insects flit about

Monday morning Craig went to work at Safe n' Sound in Flat Prairie. He expected to spend another day analyzing data from the sites of their customers in the Southwest to assess the damages. Some of these properties were completely destroyed and it was hard to get information about those properties so soon after the disaster.

Craig was surprised when his boss, Bob Meyer, suggested that he look into the proposal to install a new security system at a building in the Fort Snelling district in Minneapolis. When he opened up the folder and started reading the material he was surprised the security subcontract at Coldwater would be handled by the Halretten Group.

The only building that they wanted to install security cameras in was Building 9.

When he discussed the potential business with his boss, Craig learned that the Halretten Group wanted the system installed ASAP. They were willing to pay a premium for the job if it could be installed within ten days. Craig was intrigued to do this, because then he would have more information about both the building and the nature of the business carried on there. His boss was very eager to have this job.

:::::::

When Mencini was taken away from the hospital by the CIA agents, he was suspicious that they would want him to do some covert operation for them. However, he felt comfort in knowing that he was wanted, and as long as they had a need for him, they would help him get what he wanted: out of the country to a safe place abroad. They brought him to an office that they had in Albuquerque and soon began briefing him on an operation they were working on.

There was an opportunity during all the chaos and catastrophic earth changes for the CIA and its allies to move quickly to strengthen their positions. One of the places where they hoped to get a stronger bargaining position was with the armament manufacturers in Minnesota. It was a small but technically advanced group of vendors for the U.S. military, and having more influence there would help the CIA control military support for their covert operations throughout the world. Currently they had members of the Halretten Group working out of an abandoned building near the federal military base called Fort Snelling. Their front was that they were supervising the demolition of one of the buildings on the old campus. This group was setting up computer surveillance of the communication systems for the nearby military manufacturers. However, this was only part of the plan to get more control. What was needed was someone like Mencini; someone with the skills to infiltrate the local financial institutions supporting the military manufacturers and to create an indiscreet transfer of money that would implicate the leaders of those industries. This apparent indiscretion would compromise the integrity of the leaders and they would most likely be willing to exchange favors with the Halretten Group to remain free of criminal prosecution.

In exchange for Mencini's services, the CIA would guarantee Mencini's safe journey to Bogota, all expenses paid. In addition, as part of the covert operation, they would influence the transfer of Mencini's funds from the now flooded banks in the Cayman Islands to other banks of his choosing. He had to agree, because with the charges being held against him, he would be indicted if he didn't.

Mencini reluctantly agreed, and plans were made to get him to Minneapolis within a week or so, which would give him time to heal and also become more familiar with the details of the plan.

Craig was curious and excited about the prospect of installing security cameras at the Coldwater Spring site. He could feel goose bumps on the back of his neck when he thought about the danger involved in this endeavor. He asked his boss to have another one of the local technicians install it, and for him to be the project superintendent. He would coordinate with the Halretten Group and all of the other vendors and local utilities. Bob Meyer agreed.

Within two days they had identified enough equipment to start this project and had selected a start date, which was within the week. Craig let the contact at Fish and Wildlife know that they could meet their requirements, and they sent back a signed contract by fax within 24 hours. Craig also secretly made plans to have the information collected by the cameras sent to a data storage site at another location, where he could access it in the future. He was curious to learn more about what seemed like an unethical operation.

Meanwhile, Sally was able to get work at the Hennepin County Medical Center in downtown Minneapolis. She was delighted that she found work so fast and she started to look for a place of her own. The following Monday she was looking for places to rent in Linden Hills or somewhere nearby in the Uptown part of Minneapolis, where she would have a short commute on public transportation to the hospital.

At this time most of the public commuter buses were powered by electric motors that could operate for four to five hours before having their battery packs replaced. Every bus had a back-up battery pack and the batteries were on a pallet that could be slipped in and out of the buses at the bus garage. While they were using one pallet of batteries another would be charging. Over half of the people who had been commuting by car had stopped because of the problems with gasoline supplies. The demand for public transportation was stronger than it had ever been before, and the local transportation providers, the Met Council, had created a plan that allowed for maximum use of its existing buses. This plan was coordinated with employers, who were able to flex their schedules so that the rush hour was extended to a six hour period in the morning and a six hour period in the late afternoon and early evening.

During this same period of time, Safe N' Sound had decided to set up a satellite office in the city because they had so many clients there and transportation to and from the city had become more expensive and less reliable. Craig was asked to operate out of the metro area, and he also looked for a place to rent. Since the Safe N' Sound was able to locate to an office warehouse in St. Louis Park, he was looking for a place near the Uptown area also. Within days, Craig found an apartment that would meet his needs off of Lagoon Avenue just east of the Lake of the Isles. He was delighted to learn that Sally also had found an apartment in that neighborhood. She had found an old house with two apartments, and she rented the one on the main floor.

::::::

Meanwhile, Mencini had arrived in Minneapolis and began learning his role to get owners and operators of military equipment manufacturing financially compromised. One of the groups he would visit would be the Group at Building 9.

The operation at the Coldwater Spring building included a group of internet hackers, who had been working to get banking and financial information about the key players they had targeted. They simultaneously were working on a plan to create a movement of funds that would implicate the key players for embezzling or some other act of indiscretion. This was possible with Halretten Group operatives working within the banking system. The Main Street Bank was one of the places where a few of the manufacturers did business, and there was a group operative working in the oversight department of that bank. This individual had access to special codes and other information.

By the time Mencini visited the Coldwater Spring area, the Safe N' Sound technician had installed most of the camera system and was working on hooking the system up to the building's communication wiring system. Because the building had been vacated for so long, a lot of new wire had to be installed. It was during this installation that Craig's technician was able to find a telephone wire that could be activated to a remote site. Since Craig knew a lot of telephone company personnel from all his previous installations, he was able to coordinate with one of the telephone company personnel for the use of one of those lines for test purposes. This allowed him access at a remote site via his laptop computer and a telephone hookup. He was given a special number to call that would put him in direct contact with the security system at Building 9.

Craig also had the technician install a few boxes with microphones with the cameras. This was easy to do because they were often part of the security systems; they simply had to be activated.

When Mencini entered Building 9, his movement was recorded onto the system memory. Later that week when Craig was reviewing the recordings, he saw and recognized Mencini.

'Oh my god! It's him!' Craig could feel goose bumps on his arms and the back of his neck. 'I was right. There is some evil underway here. Wow! I can't believe the man that robbed us of the pickup truck in Arizona is involved here.'

Craig next backed up the system and played what recordings they had. He could hear sporadic parts of the conversations, phrases like, "He's the mark," and "This will play out in the contact operation," and "That's good. Numbers like that will certainly implicate him." He also learned that the highway robber from Arizona's name was Al. Overall, however, Craig had no idea what they were up to, but he did get some names like Duelatron, and Aerospace Systems, and Placer Recovery Systems. He decided to look up information about them.

Craig looked for each of the names on some internet search systems and learned that they were all companies that produced equipment or supplies for the military. He sensed that something sinister was being planned, but he still did not know what was going on and why there was this covert operation which involved a man with no scruples, such as the highway robber named Al, from Arizona.

Craig brooded on this problem for a while. He thought of telling someone at the police force, but he really didn't have any evidence other than his suspicions and his story about Arizona, and he doubted that the police would take that seriously.

There were a number of places where Safe N' Sound had security devices installed in downtown Minneapolis. One of them was at the Main Street Bank, which had an office at Marquette Avenue and Seventh Street. Within a couple days after Craig checked the Building 9 recordings, he was downtown checking the recordings of security systems at the Main Street bank and he saw Al in both the entryway cameras and at the desk of the bank receptionist. He decided to contact the branch manager and have a conversation with her to see where that might lead.

Her name was Sue Morgan and she was glad to meet with him to discuss the security system. Craig stopped in at the office at a pre-scheduled time and went over some standard explanations about the system, potential upgrades, and other routine details.

Sue's office had a large window that looked out onto Marquette Avenue. Her desk was cluttered with stacks of papers.

Briefly into the conversation, Craig asked her if anybody did any reviews of customers that came through the door.

"Sometimes we do. Why do you ask?" Sue replied as she pushed her glasses up on her nose.

"I couldn't help but notice when I was reviewing some recent activity that one of the people that came into your bank looked a lot like someone I think might have a criminal record and is perhaps a fugitive."

"That's curious," She said. "Maybe I should have our security manager review that section with you."

Craig was delighted. That was exactly the response that he had hoped for. He was even more delighted when Sue was able to call the security manager, Joe Smith, who was able to meet with Craig immediately. They went into Joe's office where several monitors were lined in front of Joe's desk. Craig sat down on the same side of the desk as Joe, and he explained to Joe what he had said to Sue. Joe started up the system and backed it up to the time frame that Craig had earlier reviewed. When they got to the frames with Al in them, Craig pointed him out. Joe was then able to capture a profile of Al and send it via internet to the Hennepin County Sheriff Department where he was able to leave a file of the profile with a deputy there.

"It will be a while before they pull an identity at their office. I'll let you know what we find out. It's really great what we can do with this technology. We rarely do this, but the bank's policy is that when ever there is any suspicion we should at least check it out."

Craig thanked him for following through and they exchanged business cards.

That evening Craig met Sally for dinner at the Chino Latino restaurant on Hennepin Avenue just north of Lake Street. Sally had been working odd hours and they hadn't seen each other for a few days. It felt wonderful for him to be with her, and he was happy to just spend time with her. They could do a lot of communicating now without talking. Yet he was anxious to tell her what he had been up to.

It was snowing, and the gentle undulating path of the falling snowflakes added charm to the street scenes outside of the restaurant where they sat. They were enjoying each other and their conversation had become shared thoughts. Because of the telepathic phenomenon they didn't have to talk. They held each others hands across the top of the table and looked into each other's eyes.

When the time felt right he started to think, 'While reviewing the security cameras at the Coldwater Spring Building 9 site, I saw what looked like that man who robbed Standing Bear and me after the earthquake in Arizona.'

'Here in Minnesota?' Sally didn't believe him at first.

'Yes. Here in Minnesota at the Coldwater Spring area, and that is what I thought. I was astounded. The fact that he was involved in the covert operation going on there added more credence to my belief that there is something very wrong that is going on there. What was even more astounding was when I saw him again on the security camera's backup system at the Main Street Bank. I told the security manager there and he sent a copy of the fellow's face to the county sheriff for a background check.' Craig was feeling a little smug to have been influential in notifying the local authorities. 'We'll find out in a couple of days just who the guy is and why he might be here in Minnesota.'

Sally coughed before expressing her concern. 'Well, I hope you don't get too involved. I don't want you to get in danger again like you did the day you planted the crystal at Coldwater Spring.'

'Yeah, there shouldn't be any reason why I would have to get involved,' Craig agreed. 'If they find out he is wanted or a felon or something, they will deal with it at the bank, I suppose.'

::::::

Craig waited two days before he called Joe Smith. "Just curious, but did you get any information back from the Hennepin County police, yet?"

"Yeah, we did. The fellow's name is Al Mencini and he is not wanted for any thing, but has been involved with some unusual activity in the past."

"Like what kind of activity?"

"Apparently there was a Ponzi scheme that happened in the Phoenix area a few years ago, and Al was implicated because of his dealings with one of the perpetrators, but never proven guilty of any involvement."

"Hmm. They didn't say what the main perpetrator of the Ponzi scheme's name was, did they?"

"Yes, in fact, they did. It was Frank Gray."

Craig was shocked and he didn't realize that he had stopped breathing. He had reacted so strongly to the news that he had a hard time responding.

"Well - ahh - uh, thanks." And he hung up the phone. He sat there in shock for a bit and when he realized he had stopped breathing, he sat there longer until he got his breath back.

Craig thought about what he had learned and all that had happened regarding the Coldwater Springs site, and he thought of Marie and Standing Bear. He decided to call his friend Standing Bear in Arizona. "You'll never guess who I've seen in Minnesota."

"Hrmm. Al Mencini."

"Let me guess; you read my mind."

"Yeah, but tell me more."

So Craig told him the whole story including the incident at Building Number 9 before his company installed the security system.

When he was done, Standing Bear said, "Hrmm. First of all, you placed the crystal at the right place. But it sounds like you may still be in danger. I'm going to talk to some of my Indian cousins in Minnesota and learn what I can about the Coldwater Spring site. I'll get back to you. Hrmm. Don't take any chances."

Standing Bear then called a friend in Minnesota, Dances With the Sky, who was very connected politically with efforts to protect sacred earth spaces in the area. The local American Indian Movement had transformed into political action groups in a more sophisticated manner in Minnesota and elsewhere. Through the wealth of the Indian gaming casinos they had become able to hire lobbyists, whose efforts included influencing politicians to help them protect sacred sites through legislation.

Dances with the Sky told Standing Bear that they had been very concerned about what was going on at the Coldwater Springs area and they were planning on taking part in a Winter Solstice event near the Coldwater Springs area. Standing Bear told them about his friends Craig and Sally and how he was concerned that the group at Building 9 was probably planning to harm them. Dances With the Sky said they were hoping to catch the group doing something wrong, which would further their cause to get the Coldwater Spring area protected. They would be watching that group and would be glad to watch out for Craig and Sally too.

After talking to Standing Bear, Dances with the Sky called leaders of the local Indian political action group. They decided to get a covert message to the Halretten Group to entice them to come to the solstice ceremony. If they did come and did anything wrong, the Indians would be ready for them.

They simply posted a poster on the gate to the Coldwater Spring area announcing that the annual Winter Solstice event would be held at the Minnehaha Falls area, since the Coldwater Spring area was gated off. This was all the information that Bert and Al needed to plan their devious plot.

CHAPTER SIXTEEN

Return to Coldwater

In the cold evening
A flock of blackbirds gather,
About one hundred.

One of the problems Mencini had been apprised of was that of frequent trespassers to the Coldwater Spring site. He was told of a recent trespasser who had drugged two of the staffers at the site. One of them was the area operations manager. Unfortunately, they had very little information about the trespasser; only one poor quality photograph. Since that incident, an improved surveillance system had been installed and all memory of multiple cameras' surveillance would be recorded. However, they had not forgotten the incident and continued to do research with the little information they had about the intruder. They especially wanted to identify him, so they could learn how dangerous to them he could be.

Although it had nothing to do with their mission, several of the staffers talked about trying to block the flow of the spring by blowing up the subterranean area. They reasoned that this would put an end to the frequent intrusions by the pantheistic groups who, in their minds, worshipped the natural earth phenomena. Personally, Mencini did not like the new age groups that used ancient ways as part of their philosophy. He found these groups to be threatening to the progressive nature of American business politics and he also considered them to be anti-religion. He was in favor of doing anything to thwart their behavior. He especially wanted to do something that would make them look unfavorable in the public eye. In the past, Mencini had always managed to keep his cool. He had always managed to stay out of public scrutiny, and he believed this was in big part due to his ability to stay unemotional and detached from the behavior of others.

This time however, Mencini was feeling very angry. He was angry that he had been forced to come up to this "god-awful" cold place called Minnesota. He was angry that he had to be involved in work that he did not want to be doing. He was angry that the CIA had him over a barrel. And he was very angry at these "new age earth-loving groupies."

'They're just going to cause more trouble,' he thought. 'We've got to teach them a lesson."

::::::

Craig would have liked to catch Al Mencini at some crime, but he did not have enough evidence. He found himself frequently thinking about possible angles and reliving the trauma of the truck heist and of the experience at Coldwater Spring. Finally one day he experienced what he called a breakdown. He became depressed and discovered in that state of mind he wasn't able to do any mind reading. He called Sally on the phone, and they chatted briefly and he told her of his problem. She came over to his place and tried comforting him, but he was out of sorts.

"I should just let the whole thing go," he confided in her. "It doesn't do me any good giving attention to Al Mencini. I need to forgive and forget."

"Let's do a ceremony," Sally offered. "You could write your negative thoughts down on a piece of paper and then we could do something of your choosing to ceremoniously let them go."

"Just like the ceremony I had years ago in Arizona."

"Yes. How would you like that to be?"

"Let's do fire again."

So Craig wrote down all his negative thoughts and they found a place in a picnic area by Lake Calhoun where there was an iron grill on a stand. They started a small fire and burnt the papers. Then Craig said a small prayer for letting go: "I pray that my negative thoughts of Al Mencini will be cleared from my mind, and that, in their place, blessed thoughts of peace and love may re-enter."

Craig felt a wave of energy come up his spine when he said this, and he felt better. Then he and Sally went out to eat at a restaurant on Lake Street on the north side of Lake Calhoun. It was in the same building as the Calhoun Beach Club and the place had last been remodeled in a contemporary theme before 2010.

They got a table by the window overlooking Lake Street and Lake Calhoun and shared some more about their lives and their hopes of having more experiences together. They talked about going up to the North Shore, east of Duluth, some weekend during the early summer next year.

When they got back to Craig's apartment they made love.

The following morning Sally had the day off, but Craig had some projects he had to work on so he put together a quick breakfast. As they sat down at the kitchen dining table to eat, Sally started reading the morning newspaper, and she noticed an article about an upcoming Winter Solstice ceremony.

"A local Wicca group and some American Indians are going to be having a ceremony at the Minnehaha Falls in the evening the day after tomorrow. I'd like to go to that. It would be fun to do, because I've never done that before and that would be my 'return to Minnesota' ceremony."

"Okay. Let's plan on it." Craig and Sally both shared a pantheistic view of nature and felt comfortable sharing an experience with local native and Wicca practitioners.

That night Craig had a dream:

He was on a plateau surrounded by mountains. There was a large flat stage that he was standing next to and immediately there began a parade of magnificent animals. Elk, bear, mountain lions, horses and other beautiful creatures were moving in front of a tall magnificent looking man, who had long beautiful hair and a wonderful cloak that flowed about his person. He was reviewing each animal and giving them encouragement.

A dwarfish man approached Craig and Craig immediately lay down. Then the tall magnificent man came up to Craig and gave him a large blue stone.

Next, Craig was overseeing a pen of cattle that he was responsible for. In the pen, the livestock were starving and it took Craig a lot of energy to bring them food, but it was not enough to allow them to prosper. So Craig decided to let the cattle out of their pens, so they could roam and graze out onto the plateau and into the valley below. The result of that action was that the cattle prospered and multiplied.

The dream was vivid and Craig remembered it in great detail. He was not sure what it meant, but it seemed and felt like a good omen.

The next day Standing Bear called Craig and asked him if there were any new developments.

"Not really. Sally and I are going to the Winter Solstice ceremony by Minnehaha Falls tonight; just north of the Coldwater Spring area. I am a little concerned about being that close to the Halretten Group. What do you think?"

"Hrmm. You're right to be concerned. There is a strong chance that the Halretten Group will be watching the people at the Winter Solstice ceremony since it is right next to where they are running their covert operation. I've been talking with my contacts in Minnesota and they plan to indirectly inform the Halretten people hoping they will come and cause a problem. That way they will have an opportunity to make the Halretten people look bad and further the cause to have the Coldspring site protected and made available to public use."

"Then maybe we shouldn't go to the event."

"I strongly believe you should be there, Craig. It would help the effort to protect the sacred spring site. Who knows, you could end up playing a pivotal role. There will be some of my friends at the event, so you should be okay," Standing Bear said, tongue-in-cheek.

::::::

Craig decided to tell Sally what Standing Bear had told him.

"What? You're crazy to go there then." Sally coughed a couple times. She was obviously upset. "We're crazy to go there. Let's not push our luck. The one close call was enough."

"But Standing Bear said he thought I should be there."

"I don't care what Standing Bear said," Sally was raising her voice now. "What about us? If you get in trouble again, you might get hurt or killed. Those people are dangerous. I can't believe you are only concerned about what Standing Bear says."

"I feel as though I would be letting them down if I stay away, now that I know what is at stake."

"What about your recent effort to become detached from your anger towards Mencini? Wouldn't an incident at the ceremony just cause those old negative feelings to come back?"

"But I am detached now, and as long as I am detached from the outcome, if I take action towards a useful purpose, I will be taking the right action."

Sally was silent for a long moment. She knew Craig wanted to go to the ceremony and she was thinking about whether or not she would join him.

"This is so ironic," she said. "The only reason this has come up is because I wanted to go to the ceremony. Now I'm thinking we shouldn't go, and you want to go." She let out a great big sigh. "Okay, I'll go with you," she said with a cough. "I hope we don't regret it."

That evening, when they got to Minnehaha, they were able to park at the lot on the north side of the falls. They couldn't see any activity, but there were a lot of cars parked there. When they got out and walked around the food court pavilion and towards the falls, they could then see where a crowd of about 100 people had built a fire down below the falls, and by taking the stairways down, they were able to approach the ceremony.

There, in the cavernous area of the river bed below the falls close to the bridge that goes over the river below the falls, the group were involved in their ceremony around the fire. The shadows of the tree branches created by the bonfire's flames danced along the cliff faces.

::::::

Al Mencini and the other man in the dark suit, Bert, who had earlier been Craig's antagonist, were among a small group from the Halretten group who had decided to stalk the Winter Solstice ceremony. There were two stealth photographers with infra-red cameras with telescopic lens, who were strategically hidden in two areas that included a spot where everyone coming down the stairways could be photographed. If 'that fellow,' who drugged two fellows from the group, came to this event, they would know about it. Not only would he be photographed, but via wireless phone the information would be transferred to Bert's laptop, which he sat viewing comfortably in the heated car with Al.

They were looking for the identity of anyone who they might already have in their file of previous trespassers at the Coldwater site. Their plan was to take that person aside and intimidate them, so that that person would spread the word to stay clear of the Coldwater site and any Wicca ceremonies remotely close to the site.

When they were able to identify someone, who looked like the man from a few weeks ago, they decided they would grab him away from the crowd. They just patiently sat in their car. The two photographers eventually left when it looked like no more people were coming and they were told that a marked man had already been identified.

::::::

When Craig and Sally came walking down the stairs, they had no idea they were being watched. They knew that there were some of Standing Bear's friends there, but they didn't know who they were or where they were. These Indians had dealt with organized government people stalking their ceremonies before and they also were on the lookout. They were aware of the intruders and were keeping an eye on them.

Craig and Sally joined the ceremony, and did their best to get downwind from the fire so they could feel some of its heat. After about an hour the ceremony was finished and the group started making its way up the creek and towards the steps. Craig and Sally were in the middle of the pack and they slowly made their way up the steps. When they got to the area next to the pavilion, the group started separating with some people going to the left of the pavilion and others going to the right. Craig and Sally chose to walk to the right of the pavilion as that was the shortest distance to their car.

Al stayed in the car when Bert got out. Bert was walking around in the wooded area above the falls and below the parking lot when the group started exiting the stairways area. Meanwhile, they had called for another group to come and help. The plan was to drug Craig and it would be easier if there were three or four of them to toss him in the back of one of the cars.

As Craig and Sally approached the parking lot, Bert started walking towards him obliquely from the left. Craig immediately sensed that this man was after him. He could see a red aura about the man and heard the thought, 'I'll have the son-of-a-bitch in a moment.'

Craig immediately put his hand in his pocket, grabbed his keys, took them out and put them in Sally's coat pocket.

'Here,' he thought. 'Take these keys and go start my car. Leave if you think you're in danger. This man is after me.'

He started moving quickly to the left so that Sally could escape.

Sally didn't need anymore explanation. She too could hear the man's thoughts and, instinctively, she quickly moved to the right.

"What the hell?" Bert muttered as he chased after Craig, who was cutting in front of him and moving very quickly.

Meanwhile, the Indian dragnet had seen what was going on and they also started to move quickly towards the perpetrator.

Craig had unknowingly started heading right towards the car that Al Mencini was sitting in. Bert picked up his pace and started running. Al saw Craig coming towards him, and it looked as though Craig was going to run right alongside his car. He decided to wait until Craig was too close to stop and then open the door and knock him down.

Al was still feeling angry and when he saw Craig running towards him, he thought of all the trouble he had been through. He was thinking, 'This bastard is just the kind of fellow who is making this job more difficult than it has to be.'

As Craig approached the car he could sense that the man inside was thinking of clipping him with the door, so he sidestepped it just in time. Al opened the door too late to hit Craig. The light came on inside the car. Craig had slowed down enough to look, and he saw Al.

"Oh, my god!" he exclaimed as he faltered.

At that moment, Al was quickly getting out of the car and hoping to grab Craig.

Craig had come to a complete stop to regain his balance after the quick sidestep. He saw Al getting out of the car and looking fiercely at him. In that instance he felt a surge of anger and he stepped towards Al, and hit him square in the face, just below the nose, with the palm of his hand. Craig could feel the impact on his hand and in his shoulder.

Al fell back towards the car and hit the back of his head on its body. His nose bleeding, he slumped down onto his knees.

Right after that moment Bert caught up to Craig, grabbed him, and instantly covered his face with a Sevoflurane ether soaked cloth. Craig collapsed unconscious from the drug.

A second later four Indian braves came out of the night and grabbed Bert. There was a brief struggle, but the Indians were not only strong and prepared to deal with Bert, they outnumbered him. They had also called the police who had been nearby. It was only a five-minute wait before they arrived.

Al was on his knees after being hit and was holding his face with one of his hands, and his chest with the other. He was having a difficult time breathing and he had a pain in his chest.

Sally had made it to their car, got inside, and anxiously watched the commotion in the direction Craig had gone. However, the other men from the Halretten group were watching her, but so were other Indians. When men from the group decided to move in on Sally, five more Indians showed up to protect her. The Halretten group backed off and left when the police arrived.

One of the Indians, who had walked up to help Sally was Dances With the Sky. Through the car glass, he introduced himself as a friend of Standing Bear.

"You know Standing Bear?" Sally was surprised and scared.

"Yes. He called me and asked that we keep an eye out for you and Craig."

"Well, I'm glad you did!" Sally was still suspicious.

"I hope Craig is okay."

"Let's go find out."

Sally paused for awhile. She looked down and centered herself calmly. Then she heard the Indian's voice in her head, 'It's okay. I am who I say I am."

She looked up and out of the window at Dances With the Sky and he smiled gently. Then she felt all right about him and she got out of the car and walked with him and one other Indian towards the police. The remainder of the Indian group continued to guard Craig's car.

The fellows from Halretten, who had been captured by the Indians, were taken away by the police and charged with kidnapping.

An ambulance was called for Craig and Mencini. They were both put on litters and into the ambulance. Craig had already come to, but for caution's sake, he was to go to HCMC for more testing. The ambulance headed towards Hiawatha Avenue and HCMC in downtown Minneapolis. But when it got to the intersection of

Minnehaha Avenue and 46th Street, it encountered an accident. A truck that was coming from the right, hit the traffic control light standard and the large lamp-holding arm came crashing down on top of the ambulance. The ambulance was frozen in place.

Sally and Dances With the Sky walked back to Craig's car and then got in the car and followed the ambulance. They were about three cars behind the ambulance when the accident happened. Sally was shocked to see the lamp post fall on the ambulance. She started screaming.

"Please try to stay calm," Dances With the Sky said as he started to get out of the car. "I'll go see if the people in the ambulance are okay."

"Oh please God, oh please let them be okay." Sally was crying.

Dances With the Sky discovered that the lamp post had fallen on the ambulance enough to make the vehicle immobile and badly damaged, but not enough to hurt any of the passengers.

Although they called for another ambulance, it would be over 30 minutes before one came. This was an anxious time. Meanwhile, Sally walked over to the damaged ambulance and was waiting for what would happen next. She spent time visiting with the other people at the scene.

Mencini was in very critical condition with major cardiac arrest. The medics did what they could, but he soon flat lined and died.

Craig, however, just needed to be watched until he came out of the anesthetic-induced trance.

By the time the other ambulance came, the medics had decided that Craig could be released, and they didn't need an ambulance for Al Mencini; a funerary would suffice. The truck driver who had lost control and hit the traffic control light, was carried away in the relief ambulance. He had a stroke and was in poor physical condition.

Yellow snow started falling. The atmosphere was still infested with ashes laden with sulfuric acid; this had turned into a form of sulfur that attached to the precipitation. The snow fall turned into a snow storm. It would end up being a long winter.

CHAPTER SEVENTEEN
Redemption

Waves lapping the shore,
Pushed by a northerly wind,
Pile foam onto the beach.

Craig's boss was upset when he learned of Craig's involvement with Halretten, how he had trespassed and drugged the Halretten employees. Craig spent a good part of the following day at the downtown Minneapolis police headquarters. His attack on Al Mencini and Al's ultimate death caused Craig to be accused of manslaughter. After much questioning he was released and scheduled for a hearing in the near future. Although Craig's story about the Arizona roadside theft and other accusations about Mencini were not solid evidence, it was the truth. The police were inclined to believe Craig and there were several witnesses that Craig was being pursued and attacked by the Halretten group. The right to protect oneself from violence from another person would give Craig enough of a defense to be acquitted of the manslaughter charge. Nevertheless, in the days immediately following the incident, Craig became very depressed. Although his attack on Mencini may have been warranted, his self-loathing for responding to his anger was overwrought.

There was a backlash after the Winter Solstice incident at Minnehaha Park for Halretten also. For one thing, political pressure was put on legislators to stop the occupation of Building 9 and the covert activity at the Coldwater Spring site. Within a few months, it finally became law that the property would become a national monument. This is exactly what the environmental activists. including the local Indian lobby. had been after for twenty years. The transition was accepted when the Minneapolis Park System agreed to add the area to their Minnehaha Park after the transition. Plans were made to finish the demolition of the remaining buildings and Coldwater Springs would finally become a protected park area.

Halretten was given 12 months to remove all the buildings and hazardous materials at the site and then leave. Their covert plans to blackmail defense equipment manufacturers went awry. And not only because they lost Al Mencini, but also because the ability of people to read each other's thoughts created a number of occasions when people in the banking system were able to catch the errors in the finance system that were necessary to facilitate a false money transfer. The clairvoyance of these people staved off all covert efforts by the Halretten Group.

During this time there were a number of economic problems *(see footnote, page 133)* with other industries as well. Safe N' Sound had several challenges trying to maintain their remote sites. One of the biggest challenges was collecting accounts receivable. The result of these problems was a decrease in income and the necessity to cut back on expenses.

Craig was laid off and Sally agreed to let Craig move in with her, and that helped Craig to exist on unemployment payments.

The weather was gloomy and the economy was depressed, but during these difficult times many marvelous and wonderful moments occurred.

Eventually Craig overcame his depression and he decided to forgive himself for his response. Once again Craig decided to honor his true self and accept his reactions to stressful situations. He decided to embrace his response and celebrate the way the events at Coldwater Spring happened. Very soon after that decision, he felt a wonderful sense of peace.

Immediately following his decision to forgive himself, Craig woke up one night as he was experiencing a wonderful light presence. As he lay there in glorious rapture, he was feeling a love that was touched by greatness. After awhile the grand aura subsided and he fell into sleep again.

When he awoke the next morning his entire sense of being had changed. Once again he felt as though he had gone through a spiritual transformation. For one thing, he could see an aura around everything, especially Sally. She had already gotten out of bed and was in the kitchen making a morning tea. She was glowing a most beautiful peach and yellow color.

Craig was excited in a quiet way. He was enjoying this new found sense of awareness and he wasn't awake very long when he started thinking, 'Oh wow, this is wonderful.'

'What's wonderful, dear?' he could hear Sally thinking.

'Everything has a beautiful aura around it.'

'Oh, and what color is my aura?'

'Peach and yellow.'

'Well, that's great, because I am feeling just peachy myself,' she giggled.

Sally suggested they take a walk around the lake before breakfast, and Craig was eager to do that. He wanted to see what the world looked like from his enlightened point of view. As they were walking across the street to get to the lake, a fast-moving commuter got uncomfortably close to Craig and he was startled. Immediately he noticed his ability to see the auras of the trees and birds and people had been greatly diminished.

When he pointed that out to Sally she said, "Oh, you've just become more grounded. You knew it wasn't going to last."

"Yeah, you're right, but I wanted it to."

For a period of time afterward, Craig began to feel a wonderful sense of love for his life. He became even more appreciative of the little gifts in his life like his daily food and water as well as the big gifts like Sally. He felt more alive than he had felt since he was a child. More than ever before he honored the feelings he felt in his heart and used that guide to make choices that would best serve his awareness of the world.

The summers were very cool and mostly cloudy, but there was an occasional day when the sun would shine through for a while and the weather would be pleasant. On just such a day while Craig was doing some yard work in the back of Sally's place, a crow flew into the yard and landed.

Craig noticed the crow and went on about his chores. After a moment he decided to sit and rest in the sunshine. While sitting there he began to think about a problem he had at work when he heard a voice in his head that said, "Never mind your work. Enjoy this moment." At first he attributed it to his spirit guide teaching him. However, the crow was still nearby and while the crow looked at Craig and cocked his head to one side, Craig heard in his mind, "Okay?"

Craig thought he would have some fun and thought to the crow, "Are you teaching me today?"

And he heard, 'Look up and, in your mind, soar above the clouds, if you want a clear view of your potential.'

And at that moment the crow looked up and then lifted off the ground and flew up into the sky above.

Craig decided to pause and to meditate and immediately felt an overwhelming sense of peace. As he meditated he imagined what he needed for food and comfort that day. He imagined a chicken dinner with vegetables and apple pie. He imagined a comfortable and warm kitchen to share with Sally and his daughter, who had moved in with them.

Later he was in the house when Sally returned from her shopping expedition. She was enthusiastic because she had the most fortuitous day. She had returned with all the ingredients for a fine chicken dinner, including an apple pie!

As a result of these changes, Craig felt compelled to spend more time studying art at the local galleries and working on his own sketches and paintings. He took some classes at the Minneapolis Art Institute and an area community college. While studying his new interest in the art world, he made some new friends.

CHAPTER EIGHTEEN
Peace and Harmony

The dove swoops unto
The branch of the old oak tree
With no breath of wind.

Standing Bear was excited as he drove down the road towards the address that Craig and Sally had given him. He had rented an electric car at the airport and had driven through Long Lake, turned north on the avenue and headed up to county Road 6, turned left and then went a short ways to Pioneer Road, which was to his right. Marie & Amel were with him.

Craig and Sally were living on a place in the country on the edge of the city. From their small farm next to a woods they could see a lake from the hilltop behind their house. They were in a farming neighborhood next to a wildlife protected area. One of their neighbors had an organic dairy, which had a herd of very healthy cows that were allowed to roam a large pasture.

One of the friends that Craig had made in the Minneapolis art world had purchased this farm in Medina and had started a vineyard on it. He offered Craig a chance to become a partner in developing the small farm into a larger vineyard. The grapes could be sold to local wineries that would make the wine. Part of the plan was to sell the farmhouse and a two-acre yard to Craig. The rest of the plan was for Craig to gradually get a growing percentage of the vineyard as he helped with planting vines and caring for the plants through the years.

Craig and Sally were fortunate that they had saved enough money to be able to make a substantial down payment and Craig's friend made the price affordable. This beautiful setting would become their permanent home. Meanwhile they both still had their jobs in the city. It was only a 25-minute drive to HCMC for

Sally. Craig had found work also as a security technician for the Minneapolis Institute of Arts.

After buying the farm, they decided they wanted to have a celebration and many old friends were invited.

The Arizona group arrived with the sun shining and the grass a vibrant green in the pasture they passed as they drove up the hill on the driveway to the farm. There were several people sitting at picnic tables in the shade of a clump of oak trees in the front yard. Standing Bear parked the car close to the picnic tables and they got out.

"Hey, good to see you guys!" Craig greeted them enthusiastically as he got up and waved one arm. He started walking towards them.

"What a fine looking group of people you are," Craig was beaming.

"It's all the good Minnesota sunshine and fresh air," Marie exclaimed.

"Hrmm. It feels good to be in Minnesota," Standing Bear joined in. "I haven't been here for a long time, and I've never seen it looking so good."

"I've never been here before." It was Amel's turn now. "And I have to admit that with the sunshine and white puffy clouds, and the many shades of green, it is gorgeous."

Sally had been in the house but now came out with a basket of food. "Hey, glad to see you finally made it!" she shouted as she walked towards the picnic tables.

There were people from Sally's family and Craig's family and friends from work and their past all gathered to help Craig and Sally celebrate the end of the long winter and the hope for a more prosperous time.

And the party went into the evening and past sunset. Many stories were told and laughs shared.

Craig and Sally had prepared places for all of the visitors, who needed a place to sleep.

::::::

In the morning, while the guests are still asleep, Craig walks up to the summit of the large hill that their farm is located on.

There is an early morning haze that creates a calm mood. As Craig works his way through the woods to the top, he frequently stops and gazes across the valley and relishes the view. That is one of the reasons why he enjoys this exercise. Suddenly, a crow caws to herald his movement, then flies off its perch towards another place further up the hill.

By the time he reaches the top, the sun is rising, casting an orange red light across the valley and up the side of the large hill. Pausing to rest, Craig sits on a fallen tree and enjoys the moment.

FOOTNOTES

(from page 126):

The economy was hit hard from all the natural disasters, and the United States was too far in debt to borrow any more money to rebuild all the damaged areas from the earthquakes and volcanoes. Those areas would have to rebuild themselves the long, slow, deliberate way, like nature itself.

The continually overcast skies and colder-than-normal temperatures created weather conditions that made it difficult to grow most crops. Certain agriculture crops did better than others. Potatoes and barley fared well, but corn and beans did not. By the second year of the aftermath of the volcanic activity and still polluted skies, food shortages became severe. There were more areas of famine and less supply of luxury food products such as fresh fruits and vegetables in the off season. During the growing season, supplies continued to remain lower than the demand for them, and prices were several times higher, even if the produce was of poor quality.

During this time after the volcanoes, the cost of transportation had soared. Besides the shortages of petroleum products, there was also a higher cost associated with running engines because of all the particulates in the air. Spinning tumblers like those used in grain harvest equipment were attached to large diesel engines' air intake systems. This only helped to a finite degree and air filters still had to be changed frequently.

Engines that had oil-bath air filters were more efficient to run. The rising transportation costs and the difficulty growing food caused imported food prices to rise significantly.

The skies didn't clear up enough for normal weather to return for over 30 months, which included three miserable winters and two summers of poor crops. There were more acres of crops planted that could tolerate cool summers, but there wasn't enough seed to go around. The country had become so dependent on a few varieties and types of crop, that stocks of seeds for alternative plants were low. Farmers that persisted in planting their corn and beans only met with grave disappointment. During both cool summers, yields were extremely low. However, because demand for the commodities was strong, farmers got enough for their low-yielding crops to pay the expensive costs of running their diesel engines.

After the 30-month period of volcanic ash contaminated atmosphere, the economy had changed. Large, energy-hungry equipment and operations that needed that kind of equipment had shut down and demand for the equipment had been drastically reduced. Instead, both farm and factories that had built-in efficiencies of scale began to thrive.

The economy had become an economy based on efficiencies. In all aspects of industry, environmental sensitivity was balanced by high costs of energy. Energy efficiencies were gained both through natural energy sources and more efficient use of space. Environmentally efficient design was the new norm for architectural and engineering standards.

There were far fewer cars and more mass transit, all predominantly powered by electric motors and hydrogen generated motors. Diesel was still used to move heavy equipment like trains and trucks, but the costs were higher. This resulted in fewer items being imported and exported from across long distances.

There just wasn't as much money around. The 30 months of bad economy had caused a financial crisis that resulted in fewer options, more unemployment, and higher taxes on those who did work. Shortages of different commodities had caused an inflation of prices. This coupled with less opportunity resulted in less available money, so the prices for many major capital expenses like land and buildings were depressed.

GLOSSARY

The following definitions were taken from Wikipedia in the fall of 2009:

The **American Indian Movement** (**AIM**) is a Native American activist organization in the United States. AIM gained international press when it seized the Bureau of Indian Affairs headquarters in Washington, D.C., in 1972, and in 1973 had a standoff at Wounded Knee, South Dakota, on the Pine Ridge Indian Reservation. AIM was founded in 1968 by Dennis Banks, George Mitchell, Herb Powless, Clyde Bellecourt, Harold Goodsky, Eddie Benton-Banai, and a number of others in Minneapolis' Native American community. Russell Means was another early leader. The early organization was formed to address various issues concerning the Native American community including poverty, housing, treaty issues, and police harassment. From its beginnings in Minnesota, AIM soon attracted members from across the United States (and Canada). It was also involved in the Rainbow Coalition. Charles Deegan Sr. was involved with the AIM patrol.

In the decades since AIM's founding, the group has led protests advocating indigenous American interests, inspired cultural renewal, monitored police activities, and coordinated employment programs in cities and in rural reservation communities across the United States. AIM has often supported indigenous interests outside the United States as well. By 1993 AIM had split into two main factions, with the AIM-Grand Governing Council based in Minneapolis and affirming its right to use the name and trademarks for affiliated chapters.

The **Hermetic Order of the Golden Dawn** (or, more commonly, the **Golden Dawn**) was a magical order founded in Great Britain during the late 19th and early 20th centuries, which practiced theurgy and spiritual development. It has been one of the largest single influences on 20th-century Western occultism. Concepts of magic and ritual at the center of contemporary traditions, such as Wicca and Thelema, were inspired by the Golden Dawn.

The founders, were Freemasons and members of *Societas Rosicruciana in Anglia* (S.R.I.A.). Westcott appears to have been the initial driving force behind the establishment of the Golden Dawn.

The Golden Dawn system was based on hierarchy and initiation like the Masonic Lodges, however women were admitted on an equal basis with men. The "Golden Dawn" was the first of three Orders, although all three are often collectively referred to as the "Golden Dawn". The First Order taught esoteric philosophy based on the Hermetic Qabalah and personal development through study and awareness of the four Classical Elements as well as the basics of astrology, tarot divination, and geomancy. The Second or "Inner" Order, the *Rosae Rubeae et Aureae Crucis* (the Ruby Rose and Cross of Gold), taught proper magic, including scrying, astral travel, and alchemy.

Ley lines are hypothetical alignments of a number of places of geographical interest, such as ancient monuments and megaliths. Their existence was suggested in 1921 by the amateur archeologist Alfred Watkins, in his book The *Old Straight Track.*

The existence of alignments between sites is easily demonstrated. However, the causes of these alignments are disputed. There are several major areas of interpretation:

- *Archaeological:* A new area of archaeological study, archaeogeodesy, examines geodesy as practiced in prehistoric time, and as evidenced by archaeological remains. One major aspect of modern geodesy is surveying. As interpreted by geodesy, the so-called ley lines can be the product of ancient surveying, property markings, or commonly travelled pathways. Numerous societies, ancient and modern, employ straight lines between points of use; archaeologists have documented these traditions. Modern surveying also results in placement of constructs in lines on the landscape. It is reasonable to expect human constructs and activity areas to reflect human use of lines.

- *Cultural:* Many cultures use straight lines across the landscape. In South America, such lines often are directed towards mountain peaks; the Nazca lines are a famous example of lengthy lines made by ancient cultures. Straight lines connect ancient pryamids in Mexico; today, modern roads built on the ancient roads deviate around the huge pyramids. The Chaco culture of Northwestern New Mexico cut stairs into sandstone cliffs to facilitate keeping roads straight.

- *New Age:* The ley lines and their intersection points are believed by David Cowan to resonate a special psychic or mystical energy.

Pantheism (literally "belief that God is all") is the view that everything is part of an all-encompassing immanent God and that the universe (nature) and God are equivalent. Pantheism promotes the idea that God is better understood as an abstract principle representing natural law, existence, and the universe (the sum total of all that was, is and shall be), rather than as a transcendent and especially anthropomorphic entity. Pantheists thus do not believe in a personal god; rather, they refer to nature or the universe as God.

Pantheism is a metaphysical and religious position. Broadly defined it is the view that (1) "God is everything and everything is God ... the world is either identical with God or in some way a self-expression of his nature" (Owen 1971: 74). Similarly, it is the view that (2) everything that exists constitutes a "unity" and this all-inclusive unity is in some sense divine (MacIntyre 1967: 34). A slightly more specific definition is given by Owen (1971: 65) who says (3) "'Pantheism' ... signifies the belief that every existing entity is, only one Being; and that all other forms of reality are either modes (or appearances) of it or identical with it." Even with these definitions there is dispute as to just how pantheism is to be understood and who is and is not a pantheist.

There possibly are three divergent groups of pantheists:

- Classical pantheisim, which is expressed in the immanent God of Kabalistic Judaism, Hindusim, Animism, Monism, Neopaganism, and the New Age, generally viewing God in either a personal or cosmic manner.

- Biblical pantheism, which is expressed in the writings of the Bible with the understanding of personification linguistics as a cultural communication idiom in Hebrew language. [Isa 55:12] [Acts 17:28] [Ps. 90:1].

- Nauralistic pantheism, based on the relatively recent views of Baruch Spinoza (who may have been influenced by Biblical pantheism) and John Toland (who coined the term "pantheism"), as well as contemporary influences. Naturalistic pantheism, founded by the World Pantheist Movement cannot be seen as theistic, since it employs the term *god* or *gods* as merely a synonym for *nature* and a non-sentient cosmos.

The vast majority of people who could be identified as "pantheistic" are of the classical variety (such as Hindus, Sufis, Unitarians, Neopagans, New Agers, Etc.), while most of those who self-identify as "pantheist" alone (rather than as members of another religion) are of the naturalistic variety. The divisions between the different strains of pantheism are not entirely clear and remain sources of controversy in pantheist circles. Classical pantheists generally accept the religious doctrine that there is a spiritual basis to all reality, while naturalistic pantheists generally do not and thus see the world in somewhat more naturalistic terms.

Volcanic ash consists of small tephra, which are bits of pulverized rock and glass created by volcanic eruptions, less than 2 millimetres (0.079 in) in diameter. There are three mechanisms of volcanic ash formation: gas release under decompression causing magmatic eruptions; thermal contraction from chilling on contact with water causing phreatomagmatic eruptions and ejection of entrained particles during steam eruptions causing phreatic eruptions. The violent nature of volcanic eruptions involving steam results in the magma and solid rock surrounding the vent being torn into particles of clay to sand size. Volcanic ash can lead to breathing problems, malfunctions in machinery, and from more severe eruptions, years of global cooling.

Ash deposited on the ground after an eruption is known as ashfall deposit. Significant accumulations of ashfall can lead to the immediate destruction of most of the local ecosystem, as well the collapse of roofs on man-made structures. Over time, ashfall can lead to the creation of fertile soils.

Spiritual transformation has a variety of overlapping meanings that carry distinct connotations:

- In psychology, spiritual transformation is understood within the context of an individual's *meaning system*, especially in relation to concepts of the sacred or ultimate concern. Two of the fuller treatments of the concept in psychology come from Kenneth Pargament and Raymond Paloutzian:

  ❑ Pargament says that "at its heart, spiritual transformation refers to a fundamental change in the place of the sacred or the character of the sacred in the life of the individual. Spiritual transformation can be understood in terms of new configurations of strivings" (p. 18).

  ❑ Paloutzian says that "spiritual transformation constitutes a change in the meaning system that a person holds as a basis for self-definition, the interpretation of life, and overarching purposes and ultimate concerns" (p. 334).

- In New Age spirituality, a transformation is the act of transforming the deepest aspects of the human spirit via a self-induced or a divine act.

QUESTIONS FOR DISCUSSION

1. Chapter One: Who was the first person in the story that appeared to have telepathic communication ability?

2. Chapter Two: What kind of transformation did Craig go through? What was Marie's special ability?

3. Chapter Three: Craig would have liked for his involvement with Frank Gray to end. How often do you have similar responses to problems that seem more complicated than you care to tackle?

4. Chapter Four: What was the explanation for Frank Gray's change in life choices? What is the process that Marie tells Craig to trust? What did Craig do that set himself up for changes in his life?

5. Chapter Five: When Craig was in the process of his emotional healing, what was the most troubling of his memories? Is the molestation issue what created a wedge between Craig and his wife or were there other mitigating circumstances?

6. Chapter Six: Does having the right sense of "how to live life" give us an advantage?

7. Chapter seven: Standing Bear seems to teach Craig in many ways. How do you think leading Craig into a meditation and prayer trance during a stressful situation helped Craig?

   - Shortly after the crevasse bypass crossing episode Craig realizes he has the ability to communicate telepathically with Standing Bear. What is it about their way of viewing the world that makes them candidates for this skill?

   - Mencini operates from a completely different paradigm than Standing Bear and Craig. What are some of the ways his approach to life is different?

8. Chapter Eight: What was the theory that the replacement of the ruby stone at the Chapel by the Sphinx in Sedona would

have a calming effect? What was the Hermetic Order of the Golden Dawn? (Glossary)

9. Chapter Nine: What is the law of manifestation? What helps to make it work? What emotion can block the positive effects of this universal phenomenon? What incident gave Craig a chance to realize instant manifestation and how did that help him? How was Amel a good companion for Craig on the Sedona journey?

10. Chapter Ten: Sometimes when we get close to realizing our goal an obstacle pops up. What was Craig and Amel's obstacle? What teacher allowed Craig to both realize telepathic communication and gave him encouragement?

11. Chapter Eleven: Through practice we develop skills. What things did Craig and Amel get by trusting their intuition?

12. Chapter Twelve: Marie explains that it was her prayerful attitude that allowed her to connect with Craig through telepathy. Is there similarity in those modes of communication? Marie also believes one of her dreams is a vision that she wants Craig to be part of. Why does Craig finally agree to her request?

13. Chapter Thirteen: Craig and Sally meet while traveling and they begin to know each other. What is it about this relationship that works so well? After the plane accident, what emotional state keeps Craig from using telepathy?

14. Chapter Fourteen: Crisis begets anxious times. What effect did the earth changes have on the economy? On Craig and Sally? After Craig gets the crystal planted, there were no immediate changes. What was different about the situation in Minneapolis versus the situation in Sedona? What is it about Craig's responses that tell us he has had an adventurous past?

15. Chapter Fifteen: What is it about the natural earth places that the Wicca and the Indian Group honors?

16. Chapter Sixteen: What is different from the way Mencini reacts to his anger and the way Craig reacts to his? Is Craig

the victim of his own karma? Does his being drugged compare to the way he drugged two of his antagonists? Ultimately, what brought about Mencini's downfall?

17. Chapter Seventeen: Does redemption seem shallow at this point? Is it less than you would have wanted it to be? Why do you think it is as it is? Does the dynamic of change factor into this?

18. Chapter Eighteen: Finally a storybook ending. Does the place and party feel right for Craig and Sally and all the other characters? If not, where would you put them? How does the last description in the story compare with the very first description in the story?